# INTO THE FIRE

# MIRIAM WALFISH

# INTO THE FIRE

## A NOVEL

THE JUDAICA PRESS, INC.

INTO THE FIRE – A NOVEL
© 2008 BY MIRIAM WALFISH

ISBN: 978-1-932443-96-7

Also by this author:
*The Jewel and the Journey*

This is a work of fiction. Any resemblance
of characters in this book to real people,
living or dead (except as noted in the
Author's Note on pp. 257–260),
is completely unintentional.

Editor: Roberta Chester
Proofreader: Hadassa Goldsmith
Cover design: C. Ruch
Internal layout: Justine Elliott

THE JUDAICA PRESS, INC.
123 Ditmas Avenue / Brooklyn, NY 11218
718-972-6200 / 800-972-6201
info@judaicapress.com
www.judaicapress.com

*Manufactured in the United States of America*

## Dedicated to

my mother-in-law, Dorothy Walfish (*Devora bas Yosef*), *a"h*, dearly loved and sorely missed. May she be a *melitzah yesharah* for her family, her friends and *Klal Yisrael*.

# PART
# ONE

# CHAPTER ONE

**D**aniel pushed the bakery cart with ease, its large wooden wheels rolling over the empty cobblestone street. He was heading home, having almost finished his first deliveries of the morning. His father, Mottel Sheinfeld, owned Sheinfeld's Bakery, and for over four years now, ever since Daniel had finished school, he had delivered rolls and bread to customers in the neighborhood, two times a day, six days a week. It usually took him two hours to complete the route, to cover the three-mile radius of the almost completely Jewish area of London called the "East End."

He liked this time of day. It was just after six o'clock in the morning, and the neighborhood was quiet, its streets calm and virtually empty. In a few hours, the streets would be crowded, full of the bustling, noisy presence of the thousands of Jews who made their homes and livelihoods here. Most of these Jews were Russian immigrants who had fled pogroms and persecution at the turn of the century.

There would be carts and carriages jamming the streets, delivery men unloading wooden

barrels full of herring and pickles, newspaper boys standing on street corners shouting the morning's headlines, ven-
dors hawking fruit, bagels and buttons, and delivery boys
dashing in and out of the tiny shops. Women of all ages,
holding errant children tightly by the hand, would be bargaining with the shopkeepers in Yiddish, the language of the
neighborhood.

Daniel started heading north along New Road, past the
crumbling low-rise buildings that were home to butchers, tai-
lors and watchmakers, and past the signs written in Yiddish
that advertised theatrical performances, fresh milk and dis-
counted tickets for ships bound for America. He noticed the
bright yellow poster, too – as he always did. It had been pasted
onto the lamppost almost two years ago, shortly after the
war had broken out. Big block letters declared "BE READY!
JOIN NOW," and beneath the message was the silhouette of
a British soldier brandishing a bayonet.

Daniel wondered if the poster would be taken down
now that conscription, or compulsory enlistment, had been
introduced. He knew that thousands of British soldiers had
been killed on the battlefields of the Western Front, and
he knew that the British were continuing to suffer tremendous losses at the ongoing Battle of the Somme, in France.
The British Army was growing increasingly desperate for
soldiers, and as a result the government had decided just
a few short months ago that all able-bodied British-born
men between the ages of eighteen and forty would be conscripted into the British Army.

Daniel thought about his friends. Just like him, they were immigrants – most of them from Russia. None of them was British-born, and therefore, they were all exempt from conscription. Though, Daniel had heard some rumors that they, too, might be forced to enlist if the war continued. He wondered if …

"Daniel, Daniel Sheinfeld, is that you? Is that you?" called Mrs. Finkel, interrupting Daniel's thoughts. Every morning except for *Shabbos*, Mrs. Finkel stood outside her house and watched for the appearance of the lanky, blonde-haired delivery boy. Daniel called back as he always did, "Yes, Mrs. Finkel, it is Daniel Sheinfeld. Good morning."

When Daniel drew closer, Mrs. Finkel inquired, "Daniel, Daniel, is it fresh, is it fresh?" – as if it were possible for rolls and bread baked only a few short hours ago to have already gone stale. Daniel knew that Mrs. Finkel was simply lonely, and that she just wanted someone to talk to. He answered her, as he always did, with an affable smile.

"Yes, Mrs. Finkel, the rolls are extra fresh today." He quickly gave her the rolls she had ordered and continued northward.

Daniel finished his deliveries and reached home a few short minutes later. He deposited the empty cart in the small yard at the back of the building. The bakery itself was in the basement, and the shop was on the street level. Daniel's family lived above the shop, on the upper level of the brick building. Daniel now went inside, his long legs effortlessly climbing two stairs at a time. He was as quiet as possible so as not to wake his father.

For as long as Daniel could remember, his father had worked through the night, baking and watching the ovens from six in the evening until four the next morning. When he was done, his father would head straight to the *shteibel* on the corner and *daven Shacharis*. Then he would return home, quickly eat breakfast and promptly go to sleep until three or four in the afternoon.

Daniel's mother, Esthereva, had trained Daniel and his three younger sisters, Henia, Yetta and Devora, to be as quiet as possible while their father slept. If they ever raised their voices — even slightly — their mother would admonish them with one of her stern looks.

Today, however, as Daniel headed up the stairs, he could hear the distinctly loud voices of two of his sisters, Henia and Yetta, arguing. "It's my hair bow," yelled Yetta.

"It is not! Tante Faiga gave it to me last year. Don't you remember, she said the green one was for me and that yours was the blue one," countered Henia.

"Girls, stop arguing or I will take both bows away from you," threatened their mother. Daniel could not believe his ears. His sisters and his mother were speaking so loudly, so early in the morning!

Was his father still awake? As soon as Daniel opened the door, his youngest sister, Devora, ran over to him and gave him a hug.

"Guess what, Daniel?" she said. Without waiting for him to answer, she pulled him into the front room.

"Papa didn't come home after *shul*. He is at a meeting. He

is not sleeping yet, so we don't have to be quiet, and we can talk as loud as we want, and Mama said that …" Surprised, Daniel looked at his mother, who was standing nearby.

"Is this true, Mama? Is Papa still at *shul*?" Before his mother could answer, Devora continued.

"Papa is at a special meeting, it is all about …"

Esthereva, a diminutive yet powerful presence, interrupted her youngest daughter.

"Devora, I think you have said quite enough. Now go to the bedroom and ask Henia to brush your hair."

"Yes, Mama," replied Devora quietly, as she headed out of the room.

"Mama, what is going on?" asked Daniel.

"Your father is not here," his mother replied tersely. "He will be coming home soon." Without saying anything more, Daniel's mother promptly left the room and went into the kitchen.

Daniel was left alone in the front room. He wondered what could be that important as to disrupt his father's routine of so many years. With a jolt, Daniel realized what this was probably all about.

CHAPTER TWO

"**Y**a *salimos de cativerio, a manana entrare-mos* (We have escaped from captivity, tomorrow we will return)," shouted the group of boys as they tumbled happily out of the *habra*, the local primary school. They had spent almost eleven hours sitting on small woven mats on the floor of the dark, airless room and they were excited that another day of school was finally over.

"*Adios, Gavriel* (Good-bye, Gavriel)," shouted Zakai, heading off with his younger brother in tow.

"*Adios, Zakai. A manana, Sion* (Good-bye Zakai. See you tomorrow, Sion)," Gavriel called back happily as he headed in the opposite direction. All of the boys from the *habra* said good-bye to each other and quickly dispersed.

Gavriel Florentin headed home under the clear blue eastern sky. He retrieved a handful of *pepitas*, roasted pumpkin seeds, from the small wicker basket that had held his lunch. The dark-haired boy with the lively brown eyes had walked home from school by himself for almost seven years, and he knew the narrow streets and alleyways of the old Jewish section of Salonika intimately. Gavriel could have found his way home with his eyes closed, yet he always kept them wide open, never growing tired of the constantly changing beauty of the city.

Gavriel passed the rows of the small wooden houses that lined the crowded little streets. Each front door was fashioned from either iron or wood, their intricately grilled front windows covered with basil and honeysuckle. Trellises of dark green vines and brightly colored carnations grew along their front walls, weaving almost seamlessly from house to house.

Above Gavriel's head, the upper stories and extended wooden balconies of the ancient buildings created a lattice-like canopy through which the bright sky was only partially visible. Laundry had been hung out to dry from the front porches; their splashes of color mixed with the vibrant green leaves of the fig, pomegranate and olive trees. The clothing and the leaves swayed together in the almost imperceptible breeze originating from the coast. In the distance, the White Tower, the ancient Turkish landmark, dazzled in the brilliant sunlight.

Soon Gavriel came to the Via Egnata, one of the main thoroughfares of the old walled city of Salonika. The paved street was a crowded, noisy, jumbled maze of tiny little shops, outdoor cafés, foreign banks and large hotels.

The street was full of people dressed in a vast array of styles and colors. Jewish men of all ages, many of whom were bearded, wore baggy cotton pants, loose cotton robes, fur-trimmed cloaks, high red fezzes and dark leather shoes.

Older Jewish women wore striped or floral robes and cloaks; a number of women wore long white shawls that covered their heads and faces, and others wore the *ferege*, a veil favored by Turkish women.

Soldiers and sailors, outfitted in varied uniforms, sat and ate at the outdoor cafes; laborers, wearing open jackets and sturdy wool trousers, jostled and shouted on the streets. Frenchmen, elegantly attired in finely cut European-style suits, conferred with each other about their business interests in the city.

The area was bustling with commerce. Trolleys clanged along the Via Egnata beside donkeys pulling carts laden with fruits and vegetables. Trucks and horse-drawn carriages tried to maneuver their way through traffic as *hamals*, porters, carrying loads of tremendous weight, expertly weaved in and out of the throngs of people.

Shopkeepers called to passersby, "*Vene aqui, vene aqui* (Come here, come here)." Coppersmiths, shoemakers, silk merchants, artisans and jewelers all sold their wares here. Young Jewish boys wearing small caps and short pants hawked copies of *L'Independent*, the popular French language newspaper. Jewish women hurried in and out of the shops, while their daughters, their thick dark hair fastened in braids and bows, trailed after them. Older women sat on wooden balconies high above, sipping sweet coffee and observing the street below.

Gavriel, who by now had finished almost all of his *pepitas*, turned off of the main street and headed west along one of the twisting, ancient side streets. In a few minutes, he reached the Benvenistes' house.

The large house was flanked by numerous apricot and lemon trees and boasted two large balconies. One balcony protruded from the front of the house outward onto the street, and the other one, in the back, overlooked the *cortijo*, the large square courtyard that Reina and Baruk Benveniste shared with their neighbors.

Gavriel could not remember a time when he had not lived with the Benvenistes. He had been only two years old when he and his mother, Allegra, had come to live here. Allegra had been employed as the family cook, and she and Gavriel had shared a room off the kitchen for many years.

Last year, when Gavriel was not quite eleven years old, his mother had died of influenza. Now an orphan, Gavriel remained in the house, cared for by Nina Habib, the housekeeper who had worked for the Benveniste family for half a century.

As he came to the front of the house, Gavriel noticed with surprise that the large iron gates that usually closed the house off from the street stood open. He saw that the two heavy oak doors to the house were open, as well. A large wagon was parked in front and two men, dressed in the baggy pants, loose cotton tops and turbans usually worn by *hamals*, were busy carrying household items out of the house.

After watching the *hamals* load a number of items onto the wagon, Gavriel decided to find Mrs. Habib and ask her what was happening. Were the Benvenistes selling some of their furniture? Were they sending some of their belongings to their daughter Roza, who lived far away in Athens?

Gavriel entered the house. He headed straight for the upper floor to the *varandado*, the main living room. Here, he found Mrs. Habib peering anxiously out of the window, watching the *hamals* load the wagon.

"Hello, Mrs. Habib. What is going on? Are the Benvenistes selling their furniture?"

"No, Gavriel, the Benvenistes are not selling their furniture."

"So why are the *hamals* carrying all of it out of the house?" asked Gavriel.

A shadow of sadness passed over the housekeeper's lined face. "Pay no attention to those *hamals*. Come, Gavriel, come, let's go to the kitchen. I have made you some of your favorite *bizochos*. We'll sit down together. We'll have a nice glass of cold water while you eat something and you'll tell me all about your day at school."

Mrs. Habib's vague answer did not satisfy Gavriel. As he followed the housekeeper down the hall, he was overcome with the feeling that somehow, something was about to change at the Benvenistes' house. What Gavriel did not know, could not possibly know, was how immediately and immeasurably his own life was going to be affected by this change.

CHAPTER THREE

The *gabbai*, Sruli Goldbloom, stood at the front of the crowded *shteibel*. Banging on the wooden table in front of him, he was trying to make himself heard. In a loud voice, he appealed to the men in the room, "Please let me finish what I was saying, let me just finish, and then everyone will have a turn to talk."

"*Sha, sha*, let Sruli talk, let him talk," shouted a number of men at the back of the room.

Sruli continued. "As I was saying, most of you know by now that last week, on July 6, Herbert Samuel, the Home Secretary, announced in the House of Commons that any Russian subject of military age who does not enlist voluntarily in the British Army will be sent back to Russia. We all know the war is going badly – thousands of men have been killed and the army is desperate for new soldiers. And all of us here have boys who are of military age, that is, boys who are at least eighteen years old. These boys were born in Russia, which makes them 'Russian subjects.' According to the Home Secretary, it looks like our boys are going to have to enlist. And so, I think that our boys should –"

Menachem Blau, an older man with stooped shoulders and a long grey beard, interjected. "Sruli, what are you talking about? Our boys cannot possibly join the British army! These are young boys, good *frum* boys – how could they survive life in the army? What would they eat? How would they keep *Shabbos*? My Avrumi in the army? It is unthinkable. No, it is impossible. My friends, let's leave things the way they are. This is just talk; the government won't really send our boys back. Everything could change in just a few weeks; the war could even end soon, at any time. Let's not do anything rash …" Then, from the back of the room they heard the booming voice of Hershel Katz.

"Menachem, you are completely wrong! What you are suggesting is ridiculous." Without pausing to catch his breath, Hershel continued dramatically, "The war has been going on for over two years now, and there is no sign that it is about to end soon. We can't just bury our heads in the sand and hope it all goes away. And, you may have noticed, all over the country there is increasing hostility to us foreign-born Jews. Our boys are seen as cowards, as not doing their duty. There have even been a few cases of Jews being assaulted by people on the street – people are calling us 'shirkers.' Just yesterday I saw an article in one of the local papers, *The East London Observer*, I think it was, about us, us Russian-born Jews. The writer recommended that England 'get rid of the whole lot.'"

"Hershel, you can't talk about the boys joining the army just because you read something in the newspaper that you didn't like," countered Menachem.

"Menachem, be realistic," Hershel said. "I am not only talking about the newspaper. I am talking about the entire situation. We have to make a decision now. We can't sit around and wait for our boys to get a letter in the mail telling them that they are about to be sent back to Russia and then worry about what to do. Menachem, don't you realize how dangerous this is? Russia is also at war. Russia is Britain's ally. This means that if our boys, *chas v'shalom*, were sent back to Russia, they would be forced to serve in the Tsar's army."

A sudden silence enveloped the room, and it was as if the *shteibel* itself shuddered at the mention of the Tsar's army. Most of the men in the room had grown up hearing stories of terrible deprivation and suffering that their fathers and grandfathers had experienced as forced conscripts, or "cantonists," in the Russian army. Many of the men assembled today in the *shteibel* had fled Russia so that they themselves and their sons would escape a similar fate.

"I have a much better idea," said Hershel as he made his way to the front. "I have heard that there are these 'tribunals' sort of like courts, made up of regular people, civilians, not army people. You can go to them and explain why you can't join the army, and then they give you an exemption. We could try to get exemptions for our boys; we could tell them that it would be too hard for our boys to be *frum* in the army." A number of men in the room nodded in agreement – it sounded reasonable.

"Hershel, I'm sorry to have to say it, but I don't think we

could get any exemptions," argued Sruli. "I heard all about this from Nosson Freedman, you know, the bootmaker. His two older boys, Bentzy and Yidel, who were born here in the East End, were conscripted a few months ago in the spring, right after conscription was introduced. Nosson took his boys to this tribunal and told the people there that his boys could not serve as soldiers because of religious reasons. After maybe just two minutes, the tribunal rejected Nosson's claim completely – the tribunal pointed out to him that thousands of Jewish boys and men are serving on every front, and have been since the war began. The members of the tribunal said that there was no reason why his boys could not serve, as well. Nosson told me that a number of other Jews from our neighborhood have tried going to the tribunal and they were not successful either. Just yesterday, I heard that both of the Freedman boys are in France now, on the Western Front."

"Do you have a better suggestion?" asked Hershel.

"Yes, I think I may have an idea," responded Sruli.

"So, *nu*, let's hear it already," said Hershel.

"Well," Sruli began, taking a deep breath before he continued, "some of you may have heard about these 'Pals battalions,' as they're called. What they are is a group of boys or men who get together, men who all know each other, maybe from work or the neighborhood. They all enlist in the army together, and they ask to stay together. The army usually agrees, and they put them all in the same unit. This way, they are with people they know, and it makes life in the army easier for them, more tolerable. We could do the same with our boys."

"Oh, I know what you are talking about," said Hershel, shaking his head. "You are thinking that our boys should join up with that man, what was his name? Jabotinsky. Yes, Vladimir, or Zev as he calls himself now, Zev Jabotinsky. I'll tell you, I went to one of those meetings already. He's promoting this absurd idea he has, something he calls the 'Jewish Legion.' He proposes a special regiment be established, just for Jewish soldiers. I've seen a few of his posters hanging in the neighborhood; he says he is part of something called the 'Committee for the Jewish Future.' It'll never happen – the government thinks he's a dangerous radical, and I know for a fact people don't like him or his new ideas. At the meeting I went to, people were booing and heckling him. No one took him seriously at all."

Sruli said, "Now wait a minute, Hershel, that's not what I am talking about. What I am thinking is that we ourselves, on our own, organize our boys. We try to get maybe twelve, thirteen boys from our part of our neighborhood here, boys who all know each other, and we have them all enlist together, just like those Pals battalions. They would all be together during basic training and would help each other, look out for each other."

By now, everyone in the *shteibel* was listening attentively to Sruli's words. He continued, sounding more confident. "As many of you know, the whole process takes a number of months. After you enlist, you are sent home and told to wait for further instructions. A few weeks later, you are contacted by mail and told to report to basic training. And then, basic training itself can be anywhere from four to twelve weeks long. So you see, almost four months could elapse. In four months' time, it is possible that this new law could be revoked, or even better, the war could be completely over, and all of the boys could come home."

"The boys, together? They would be able to stay together?" asked Menachem, sounding skeptical. "They could have a *minyan*, and they could help each other, watch out for each other, that is what you are thinking?"

"Exactly, that is what I am thinking," answered Sruli. "I have heard that there is a Rabbi Lipson in the army, right here on the home front, and he has made a special arrangement with the War Office. All Jewish soldiers can have kosher food while they are in basic training, and I have heard that he has also arranged for the boys to be able to leave for *Shabbos* sometimes."

"Well, it is an interesting idea," said Hershel.

"I guess, well, I guess this is worth considering," echoed Menachem.

The room became very quiet, as if each man was suddenly envisioning his own son in the khaki uniform of the British Army. Finally, Sruli looked at Mottel Sheinfeld, his neighbor and close friend, who was seated on his right.

"Mottel, you have not said anything. What is your opinion?"

Mottel spoke slowly and carefully, his voice not betraying any emotion. "The boys should enlist in the British Army. My son Daniel can not, will not, be sent back to Russia."

*Salonika*
*July 1916*

earing the traditional clothing of the married Jewish women of Salonika, the housekeeper sat in the dimly lit office at the back of the large building. Try as she might, she simply could not compose herself. "Excuse me, Mr. Capon," she said in a shaky voice as she retrieved yet another small embroidered handkerchief from her cloth bag.

"That's all right, Mrs. Habib, take your time. I know this must be very difficult for you," said Mr. Capon kindly. Mr. Capon was dressed in a European-style suit, and wore a tall red fez on his head.

"Well, as I was saying," continued Mrs. Habib as she dabbed at her eyes, "my employers, they are good people, Reina and Baruk Benveniste. I have worked for them for almost fifty years, and I can tell you, they are the kindest, most generous people I have ever met … but, *que pecado*, such a pity, Baruk Benveniste is not well anymore. He and his wife are selling their house, and they are moving away from Salonika. They are going to live with their only child, their daughter Roza, in Athens."

"And as for me, I am old now too, too old to work anymore. My eyesight is bad, I am no longer steady on my feet and I am increasingly forgetful. My younger brother and his wife have a small house in Monastir. Maybe you know the city? It is north of here. Well, they have invited me to live with them. And, you see, I cannot take the boy … I can no longer look after …" Mr. Capon nodded sympathetically.

Mrs. Habib continued, her eyes filling with tears yet again. "Oh, Mr. Capon, Gavriel is such a special, special boy. So much like his late mother, Allegra. He is so good-hearted, so good-natured. And smart! Just ask his *rubi*, his schoolmaster from the *habra* how smart he is! And, believe it or not, he actually knows English. Can you imagine? Of course, many of this new generation are learning French and Greek, but Gavriel, he wanted to learn English. He never gave me a moment's trouble, he is, he is …"

"Now, Mrs. Habib," Mr. Capon gently interjected, "I need to ask you a few questions."

"Yes, yes, of course," replied the distraught housekeeper.

"Are you certain that Gavriel has no remaining relatives in Salonika? Are you sure that there is nowhere else for him to go?"

Mrs. Habib nodded. "Yes, unfortunately, this is the situation. Gavriel's father died years ago, when Gavriel was just a baby. He was a fisherman, and, of course, I never wanted to ask, but I believe he drowned at sea. He had no family, as far as I know. Shortly after he died, Gavriel's mother, Allegra, came to live at the Benvenistes' house. Her parents were no longer alive, and she has only one sister; Perla is her name."

"Oh, the boy has an aunt! Why doesn't the boy go live with his aunt?" asked Mr. Capon.

Mrs. Habib shook her head sadly. "Mr. Capon, I know that Gavriel's mother would have liked nothing more than for her son to go and live with his aunt. But, you see, Perla was married a number of years ago and moved to England with her husband, Gedalia. He had some sort of business opportunity there, but I can't seem to remember now what it was. Of course, this would be the best place for Gavriel. After Allegra died, Perla wrote me and told me to make arrangements to send her the boy immediately, that she would wire me the money for the fare. But then we found out that ever since the war started, ordinary citizens from Salonika are not allowed to travel overseas. They say it is too dangerous. And so, I arranged with Perla that Gavriel would remain with me at the Benvenistes, and that when the war was over, I would send him to be with her in England."

Mr. Capon also had heard that civilian travel was prohibited at the moment. "Do you have an address for this aunt, this Perla?"

"Yes, yes, it is right here, let me get it for you." Reaching into her bag, Mrs. Habib retrieved a small blue envelope, the British stamp clearly visible on the upper right-hand corner. "This is one of the last letters Perla sent her sister. The return address is right here, at the top. It is 'Mr. and Mrs. Gedalia Perahia, 11, Earlscourt Lane, Leeds, England.'"

Mr. Capon came out from behind his desk and went to

take a seat beside Mrs. Habib. In a reassuring voice, he said, "This is what I think you should do. Have Gavriel come and stay here for now. We will do our best to look after him. Hopefully, the war will end soon and, once it is safe to travel again, you have my word that I will do my utmost to help Gavriel get to England."

Mrs. Habib thought this over for a moment. "You will make sure that Gavriel gets to England?"

"Mrs. Habib, I cannot promise, but I will do my very best," he replied.

The housekeeper looked slightly calmer now. "What should I do now? When should I bring Gavriel here?"

"Go home, pack up his belongings and bring Gavriel here tomorrow after lunch. But please, Mrs. Habib, you must make sure you write his aunt and uncle a letter. You must inform Perla and Gedalia Perahia where their nephew will be until the war is over – The Allatini Orphanage for Jewish Boys."

# CHAPTER FIVE

**H**is back to his son, Mottel's long, powerful arms were immersed up to his elbows in the trough of dough. Mixing the bread dough by hand was hard, backbreaking work and Mottel was sweating, stopping every few minutes to wipe his brow with his forearm. He was bare-chested; the long scar that snaked its way along his broad back was clearly visible.

His father had told Daniel a few hours ago that he wanted to speak to him, and that he should come down to the bakery later that evening. Daniel had been waiting downstairs for close to half an hour now, but he had yet to utter a single word.

Finally, his father looked up from the dough and glanced over his shoulder. Speaking deliberately and slowly, he said, "I was at a meeting today. The situation is bad, very bad. The army has lost thousands and thousands of men, and there is a shortage of soldiers. The government needs new recruits. I have been told that the government is planning to send you boys from the neighborhood, you boys who were not born here, back to Russia if you do not enlist soon in the British Army." His voice seemed to catch slightly on the word "Russia."

He continued, his voice rising slightly. "I will not let this happen." He took his arms completely out of the trough of dough and turned to face Daniel. Daniel remained silent.

His father looked directly at him. "I want to tell you something. I have never spoken of this to anyone, and I will never speak of this again. I am telling you this so that you will understand the decision that I have made."

Daniel nodded, and his father began.

"In 1881, Tsar Alexander the Second was assassinated. There followed a terrible, terrible time. Many Russians, including the new Tsar, Alexander the Third, blamed the Jews for the death of the previous Tsar. For the next three years, there were anti-Jewish riots and pogroms all over the southwestern part of Russia. The peasants, with the support of the secret police, were whipped into an anti-Jewish frenzy, and they ran through hundreds of towns, setting fire to Jewish homes and assaulting Jewish men, women and children. The government, of course, did nothing to stop them.

"One night, in 1884, a pogrom erupted in my hometown, in Kalarash, a *shtetl* about fifty kilometers north of Kishinev, where my family had lived for hundreds of years. My parents owned a small grocery store in the center of the town, and I had worked there since I was a child.

"It was the middle of December, bitter cold and very late at night. I was heading home, having stayed late at the store because large shipments of flour and sugar had been delivered that day and I needed to weigh all of it. Your mother was waiting for me at home. We were both very young, barely twenty years old, and we had only been married for a year.

"As I approached our street, I began to hear noises – strange, frightening noises. As I drew closer, the anguished sounds of men, women and children, shrieking, screaming and begging for help, became louder and louder. To my horror, I saw a group of local peasants, some of whom I had known for years, running in and out of the houses, wielding knives and shouting in Russian, 'Kill the Jews! Kill the Jews.'

"Panic stricken, I ran to our house and yanked open the door. I saw that the house had been completely ransacked. Pots and pans had been thrown to the ground, the feather beds and pillows had been slit open, furniture had been smashed, and there was broken glass everywhere. I could not find your mother.

"I charged back outside to the small yard behind the house. And there, there I found your mother, cowering in the darkness. In her arms she held our newborn baby boy.

"I moved toward her. At that second, I heard someone from behind me shout in a drunken voice, 'Coward, coward, hiding in the backyard!' I turned to see a peasant coming toward me, holding a long knife. 'Jew, Jew, what valuables are you hiding back here? Diamonds and gold? Silver coins? Jew, Jew, what are you hiding?'

"Until then, the baby had been quiet, but now he began to cry. The peasant suddenly noticed your mother, and noticed our baby, too. With a cruel smile on his face, he said, 'Oh, you're hiding a baby, a little Jewish baby. Let me take a look.' As he came closer, I felt a surge of terror. In a blind fury, I lunged savagely at the peasant, trying to grab hold of his knife. We struggled, and I fell to the ground."

His father stopped for a few minutes. The silence in the bakery was enormous, oppressive.

"I lost consciousness. When I awoke, I was lying near the burned rubble of what had been our house, and I was covered in blood. Your mother was sitting beside me, her face blank with shock. In her arms was our son ... she was still holding our son. He was quiet now – too quiet. Our baby, our Yossel, he was ... he was gone.

"At that moment, in that little yard in Kalarash, I promised myself, and I promised your mother, that I would do whatever I needed to do, no matter how difficult it would be, no matter how long it would take, to get away, far, far away, from that wretched, accursed country. And I vowed that we would never, ever return to Russia.

"It took many years, many difficult years, but eventually, we were able to buy tickets for passage to England. We were childless for a long time, and then, right before we were set to leave, you, Daniel, were born.

"We came to London via Hamburg, crammed into steerage class with hundreds of other Jews fleeing Eastern Europe. We docked at Irongate Stairs, just below the Tower Bridge, in the autumn of 1899, on a cold, wet, dreary day. The smoke from the chimneys at the docks was so thick that your mother and I thought the sky in England was grey, not blue.

"The only person we knew was Faiga, a distant cousin of your mother's. She took us in, and we lived ten to a room. We didn't speak English, we didn't know anyone and we were poor, we were very poor. At first, I worked as a peddler, selling fruit. But your mother knew how to bake *challah*, and, after a little while, we had saved up enough money to rent an oven from a neighbor. We started making *bilkas*, hundreds and hundreds of challah rolls, and sold them from an old wheelbarrow in the neighborhood. We worked twelve, sometimes fourteen hours a day.

"After seven years in this country, I was able to open our shop. When it first opened, people in the neighborhood shook my hand and said to me, 'Sheinfeld, you own your own business! Now you are a true success!' but I didn't say anything. To me, I was a success because I had managed to get my wife and family out of Russia, and I was certain that we would never have to return."

His father sighed deeply and paused for a moment. Not sure of how to continue, he slowly said, "And now, Daniel ..."

"Papa," Daniel said quietly, feeling suddenly protective of his father, "you do not need to say anything else. I know what you have decided. It is the right decision. With *Hashem*'s help, I will be fine."

The father and son locked eyes for a brief moment. And then, without saying anything else, Daniel's father turned his back toward him and returned to mixing the bread dough. Daniel silently left the bakery and slowly headed up the stairs.

*Salonika*
*July 1916*

CHAPTER SIX

"How do you do, sir? This sponge cake is lovely, thank you. I am so pleased to make your acquaintance." As he sat under the ancient olive tree in the Benvenistes' *cortijo*, Gavriel was practicing speaking English. He had been learning English for years, ever since his Aunt Perla had sent him a small book of English phrases. And soon, very soon, he believed, he would actually be in England and he would be able to speak English to everyone! He was very excited.

He had already figured out that the Benvenistes were moving. It would have been impossible for him to think otherwise. Although Mrs. Habib had remained silent on the subject, Gavriel had heard some of the servants talking. He knew by now that the Benvenistes were selling their house and were going to live with their daughter Roza in Athens, and he guessed that Mrs. Habib would go to live with her brother in Monastir. Gavriel would surely miss Mrs. Habib; she had been so kind to him all these years, almost like a grandmother. *Well*, Gavriel thought to himself, *maybe Mrs. Habib will be able to come visit me in England.* Or maybe his aunt and uncle would let him come back to Salonika to visit. By then, of course, he would be dressed like a real little Englishman, and people probably wouldn't even recognize him!

He was certain that this morning Mrs. Habib had gone to arrange a ticket for him on a boat bound for England. After all, how often did Mrs. Habib get dressed up and leave the house? He couldn't remember the last time she had gone out. And he had heard her tell the new cook that she would not be home for lunch, that she had an important meeting with a "Mr. Capon."

Gavriel also knew that Mrs. Habib had taken one of his Aunt Perla's letters with her. These letters had always been kept in a small wooden box on a shelf in the kitchen. Gavriel had seen Mrs. Habib take one out earlier this morning and put it into her bag. This was certainly to show the ticketmaster Aunt Perla's address.

Of course, Gavriel would be sad to leave Salonika, the beautiful city of his childhood. Gavriel's mother had told him so much about Salonika, its history and its people, and Gavriel knew that it was a very special place.

He knew that the port was a main trade route in the Mediterranean. His mother had told him that there had been a small Jewish community in Salonika for a long time, but that thousands and thousands of Jews had come here from Spain and Portugal. Other Jews from Sicily, Italy and Hungary had followed. His father's family, Gavriel knew, had originally come from Florence, in Italy, and that is where his last name "Florentin" had originated.

His mother had also told him that the Jewish community of Salonika grew into an important center of Torah study. It had numerous *yeshivot*, synagogues and organizations to help the needy. A few hundred years ago, a famous poet had actually given the city the nickname "*Ir V'em B'Yisrael* (Metropolis and Mother of Israel)." Although the city was home to many other nationalities, especially Turks and Greeks, the Jews had formed the largest single group in the city for hundreds of years now.

Many Jewish men worked as fishermen, and because so many Jews worked at the port, it closed early Friday afternoons and remained closed on *Shabbat*. The Jews were so involved in the commercial life of the city that all the businesses in Salonika were closed on *Shabbat* and holidays, too. Many non-Jews in the city could speak Ladino, the language the Jews spoke. Just yesterday, in fact, Gavriel had been talking to the gardener, who was not Jewish, and the gardener had used the word …

"Oh, there you are, my boy," called Mrs. Habib. "I was looking for you in the house. How are you, my dear?" Gavriel jumped up from under the tree and ran over to meet her. He saw that Mrs. Habib looked very tired. The elderly woman was clearly not used to walking around the city. "Mrs. Habib, I am fine! I am better than fine! I can't wait to hear all about your meeting this morning!"

Mrs. Habib was taken aback. She was surprised that

Gavriel seemed to know about her trip to the orphanage. She had not mentioned her meeting to anyone.

Puzzled, she asked, "Gavriel, how did you know about my meeting?"

"Oh, Mrs. Habib," said Gavriel excitedly, "I understand you didn't want to tell me everything until it was all arranged, but I heard some of the servants talking, and I know that the Benvenistes are moving and that we are no longer staying here. This morning, I heard you tell the cook that you were going to see someone named Mr. Capon, and then I saw the opened box of my Aunt Perla's letters. So I figured out that I am moving to England and that you needed the address to give to the ticketmaster, who most certainly is this Mr. Capon." Gavriel smiled brightly at Mrs. Habib.

For what must have been the twentieth time that day, Mrs. Habib eyes filled with tears.

"Mrs. Habib, please don't cry. I know you will miss me, and I will certainly miss you, too, but I will write to you, and maybe one day I will be able to come and visit you and …"

"Oh, Gavriel, Gavriel, my dear boy. You are mistaken. Mr. Capon is not a ticketmaster, he is, he is …" Mrs. Habib stumbled over the words. "Mr. Capon is the director at the Allatini Orphanage for Jewish Boys."

Gavriel's large brown eyes opened wide with disbelief. "The what? An orphanage? What are you saying? I am going to an orphanage?"

Mrs. Habib, weeping freely now, put her grandmotherly arms around the boy. Through copious tears she said,

"Gavriel, Gavriel, it is only for a short while. Mr. Capon knows all about your aunt and uncle. He has promised me that once the war is over, he will make sure you are sent to England." Gavriel remained silent, his face expressionless.

Mrs. Habib continued. "Gavriel, I have looked around the building. It is a very nice place, very cheerful, and the other boys look very happy. Hopefully, you won't be there long. You know, it could be only a few weeks, a month, and it will be safe to travel again."

Gavriel walked away from Mrs. Habib and went to sit down again under the olive tree. Leaning his head against the enormous trunk, Gavriel looked up at the countless little leaves on the branches. The leaves were swaying ever so softly in the gentle breeze, and Gavriel thought they looked like thousands of little hands, all of them slowly waving his plans good-bye, good-bye, good-bye ....

A total of twelve Jewish boys in the neighborhood had arranged to enlist together. Of the twelve, three were Daniel's closest friends – Moishe Goldbloom, Avrumi Blau and Chezki Katz. The night before they were set to enlist, the four friends sat in the Goldblooms' front room and talked about what was ahead of them.

Moishe, Daniel's next-door neighbor and closest friend, said, "Just like my father says, as long as we can stay together, we will be fine. There's twelve of us, it's a big group. I'm not worried." Moishe, a redhead, was gap-toothed, pudgy and deeply freckled. He wore a perpetual smile on his face and worked as an apprentice to a tailor. People always joked that the tailor needed to keep a close eye on Moishe. He was so good-natured he was liable to give you the shirt off his back, and one or two shirts belonging to the tailor, as well.

"I am not so certain that it is going to be as easy as you think," said Avrumi, or "Reb Blau" as his friends called him. Avrumi's friends had given him this nickname years ago when they were in *cheder* together, in recognition of his sharp mind and excellent memory. Avrumi had a medium build, neat, even features and clear blue eyes of unwavering intensity. "Even if we manage to stay together in a group, we're still going to be in the army. We are going to have to do all sorts of drills and marches, learn how to handle weapons, take orders, all kinds of things like that. It's going to be very difficult."

"I know what Reb Blau is worried about," teased Chezki. "He's worried that the army might occasionally ask him to lift his head out of a *sefer*. You know, Reb Blau, life in the army is not going to be like the place where you work, at that printer's shop, where Mr. Klein lets you sit and learn when business is slow."

Daniel interjected, "Well, Chezki, you may be right. Reb Blau may have to cut down on his learning a little bit, but what about you? You are going to have to take a break from all of your money-making schemes for a while, don't you think?"

Chezki, dark-complexioned and wiry, had a head full of dark curly hair and a mind full of plans, big plans. He was brash, he was bold and he wanted to make money. Lots of money. He wanted to get out of the East End as soon as possible and move to one of the nicer parts of London where some of the more established Jews had started to settle, like Golders Green. "Daniel, you'd be surprised. I have a feeling even in the army there's money to be made. In fact, I have an idea ...."

At that, all four friends started laughing. All of Chezki's

great schemes always started with those four little words, "I have an idea."

"Sure, sure," said Daniel, smiling his trademark lopsided smile. "Tomorrow, I think you should tell the recruiting sergeant all about your idea. I am sure he would love to discuss it with you!"

The friends continued talking for quite some time. Daniel was the first to leave; he needed to go to sleep early so that he would be able to wake up at 4 a.m. for the next day's deliveries.

The next morning after *Shacharis*, all twelve boys met at the recruiting station on Whitechapel High Street, directly across from the London Hospital. They did not have their parents accompany them, all their fathers having agreed that the sooner their sons got used to the idea of facing the army on their own, the better.

They entered the building and stood in the hall. They were not sure where to go or whom to talk to, and they looked perplexed and anxious.

A middle-aged soldier seated in the front office caught sight of the boys. He called, "Are you lot here to 'take the king's shilling'?" Without waiting for an answer he continued, "Don't dawdle out there in the hall. Come in, let's see how many of you there are."

The boys obediently filed into the office.

The soldier surveyed the group. In a low tone he said to a soldier sitting beside him, "A motley bunch, this lot. Look at that one on the side, that chubby red haired one.

He's sweating already! And that dark one over there, he looks awfully fidgety. And that other one over there in the back, whatever is he doing? Mumbling something to himself out of a tiny book?"

"Never mind, Sergeant," said the other soldier. "The army needs more men. Our job is to get them signed up so they can be shipped out."

"Yes, of course, you're right."

The soldier stood up and said, "I am Sergeant Connor. Form up over there. I need to see your documents."

The boys lined up and, one by one, they stepped forward and presented their papers. The sergeant soon realized that all these boys were Jewish, and that they lived close to each other in the East End.

"Are you lot friends, then?" he asked. Again, the boys did not know if they were expected to answer the sergeant or not. "Enlisting together, is it? Personally, I think that's a good idea. Now I can't make any guarantees, but seeing as how you lot are enlisting all at the same time, I'll try to send you to the same place for basic training." When the boys heard this, they felt a tremendous sense of relief. This was exactly what they and their families had been hoping for.

Sergeant Connor continued. "Right. Listen up. Each of you must undergo a brief physical exam. You will go to the small room on the left, and when you are done, you are to come back here." The sergeant knew that the possibility of anyone not passing the physical was extremely remote. The exam was cursory at best, and was designed to weed out only those with the most severe health problems.

"And now, leave the room in the order that you presented your papers to me: Gordon, Orenstein, Shapiro, Abramsky, Weitz, Handelsman, Kaganoff, Sheinfeld, Goldbloom, Blau, Teitelbaum and Katz."

Within minutes, all of the boys came back to the front room. Not surprisingly, all of them had passed the physical.

"All soldiers," the sergeant instructed, "must swear an oath of allegiance upon entering the army, a process we call 'attestation.' Now, I know that your religion does not allow you Jewish boys to swear an oath, so instead, you will 'declare' your attestation. Once all of you have attested, you will have formally enlisted, and you will each receive one shilling, which is symbolic of one day's pay in the army. You will then be free to go home. I expect you will be hearing from the army within a few weeks or so. At that time, you will be told where and when to report for basic training."

One by one, each boy stood before the recruiting sergeant and attested. In voices that were alternately loud, low, clear, high-pitched and, in many cases, heavily accented, each boy said:

> I solemnly, sincerely and truly declare and affirm
> that I will be faithful and bear true allegiance to
> His Majesty King George, his heirs and succes-
> sors and that I will as in duty bound honestly and

faithfully defend His Majesty, his heirs and successors in person, crown and dignity against all enemies and will observe and obey all orders of His Majesty, his heirs and successors and of the generals and officers set over me.

Daniel and eleven other boys from the neighborhood were now soldiers in the British Army.

# CHAPTER EIGHT

**W**hile Mrs. Habib was inside making a few final arrangements, Gavriel waited outside on the front steps of the squat building. He watched as two little boys played *pares y nones* (evens and odds), a game he himself had played for years.

The boys stood opposite each other, both of their right hands closed into fists. The bigger boy said, "I am evens," and the other responded, "I am odds," and then they both dropped their right hands and opened one or more fingers. The bigger boy totaled the number of fingers on both of their hands and declared with a shout that he was the winner because he had predicted evens, the correct outcome.

Gavriel noticed that the boys were dressed much like he was, in the modern style – light cloth caps, loose-fitting cotton shirts with buttons down the front, short dark trousers that ended above the knee, and leather shoes. Watching them play, Gavriel thought that these boys were proof that everything would work out and that living in the orphanage would be tolerable; after all, the boys were dressed just like he was, and they were playing the same games that he played.

As a small child, Gavriel's mother had imbued in him the knowledge that everything in life came from *Senor del Mundo* – that everything in the world, from the tiniest flower to the highest mountain, was part of His majestic creation, and that everything that happened was all part of His larger plan. She had told Gavriel that everything happened for a reason, even if we, mere people, could not perceive the reason at the moment. And so, this morning, as he stood outside of the orphanage, Gavriel felt convinced that everything would work out, that everything that had happened to him was part of *Senor del Mundo*'s plan, and that somehow, he would manage in his new, temporary surroundings.

Soon, Mrs. Habib emerged from the building with a pleasant-looking middle-aged man at her side. Gavriel assumed correctly that this was the director of the orphanage. The man approached Gavriel and said kindly, "Hello, I am Mr. Leon Capon, and you must be Gavriel Florentin. I have heard many wonderful things about you from Mrs. Habib." Gavriel nodded and smiled, unsure of how to respond. Mr. Capon continued, "Now, say good-bye to Mrs. Habib, and then I will take you inside. One of the boys will show you around."

Mrs. Habib, looking momentarily startled, quickly embraced the boy. "Gavriel, did you remember to take everything? The cookies I made for you? All of your English books? Oh my, what about your kaleidoscope? You did pack that, didn't you?" Mrs. Habib knew full well that Gavriel had taken everything because she had been the one who had overseen all of his packing just the night before.

"Now, Mrs. Habib," said Mr. Capon, in a voice that suggested that what he was about to say he had said many times before, to many different people, "I am sure the boy has all that he needs. It is best that you say a brief farewell and be on your way. Long goodbyes make it harder for everyone."

The housekeeper sighed loudly. "Yes, yes, of course, you are right. Gavriel, take good care of yourself. And don't worry; as soon as I leave you, I am going to the post office to mail a letter to your Aunt Perla, just as I told you I would. I have the letter right here in my bag. She and Mr. Capon will make arrangements for you to go to England once it is safe for you to travel."

Mrs. Habib embraced the boy one last time, murmuring *"El Senor del Mundo que mos guarde* (*Hashem* should protect us)." She slowly began to walk away from the building, frequently looking back over her shoulder until she could no longer see the dark-haired figure of the boy she had helped to raise.

Mr. Capon led Gavriel into the building. Gavriel surveyed his new, unfamiliar surroundings – the interior of the orphanage had bare white walls, colorless floor tiles and a few plain pieces of furniture. A feeling of emptiness pervaded the building.

"It is just after lunch," said the director, "and most of the boys are in their rooms right now. In half an hour, it will be time to go back to school for the remainder of the day. I will have one of the boys show you the room where you will be sleeping, and then you will go to school this afternoon with everyone at the *Habre Grande* (Talmud Torah).”

“I will go to school with the boys?” asked Gavriel, sounding surprised.

“Yes, of course, all the boys here go to school at least until their bar mitzvah,” responded Mr. Capon.

Gavriel was confused. Mrs. Habib had not mentioned going to a new school. “I will not go to my own *habra*, with all of my friends and my *rubi*?”

“Oh, no, my boy, everyone here goes to the same school. We couldn’t very well have all of you boys walking all over the streets of Salonika every morning, going to your own little *habras*, could we?” responded the director.

Mr. Capon noticed one of the boys walking in the hall. “Sebi, come here. Show this new boy around. His name is Gavriel Florentin. He will be in the same room as you. Introduce him to the other boys and show him where to put his things.” Mr. Capon then excused himself to attend to the paperwork waiting for him in his office.

Sebi was a broad-shouldered boy with the beginnings of a mustache on his upper lip. He approached Gavriel and immediately demanded to know, “What’s your story?”

Gavriel was not sure what Sebi meant. “What do you mean, my story?”

“Why are you here?” Sebi said. “Did your parents die?”

Gavriel was a little taken aback by the questions Sebi

posed, but realized that this topic must be everyday conversation in an orphanage. "My father died years ago at sea when I was a baby, and my mother died last year of influenza. I used to live with the Benvenistes but they are old and are moving away from Salonika, so I had to come here. But, really, just for a very short time. I have family in Leeds, England, and I am going there very soon."

As he led Gavriel down the corridor, Sebi repressed a small smirk. Every new boy said that he was here "really, just for a very short time."

He played along for a little bit. "Leedsengland, where is that?"

"Oh, it's a very important city; it is part of the British Empire, very far away. My aunt and uncle live there, and soon I will, too," replied Gavriel confidently.

"That's interesting," replied Sebi, continuing to smirk.

The two boys came to a large room that was crowded with row upon row of metal beds. The walls of the room had been painted a sterile white, and each bed had a single white pillow and a dark brown blanket. "This is the older boys' room. All the boys who are ten years old and over sleep here. There are eleven of us all together; well, twelve now, counting you," said Sebi. As he led Gavriel into the room he announced in a loud voice, "This is Gavriel Florentin. His father died at sea years ago and his mother died of influenza last year."

Gavriel felt ten pairs of eyes looking at him intently. For a brief second, Gavriel felt strangely, unusually self-conscious.

"You can take the empty bed in the back corner, and

there is a shelf against the back wall where you can put your things." With that, Sebi disappeared. It was clear that he felt that he had better things to do with his time.

Gavriel went over to the empty bed and opened his bag. At the top were his two most treasured possessions, the photograph of him and his mother, taken about two years ago, and his kaleidoscope, a birthday gift his Aunt Perla and Uncle Gedalia had sent him when he had turned eight. He was reluctant to leave these things on the shelf, out in the open for all these boys to look at. He decided to leave the photograph and the kaleidoscope inside his bag for the time being.

A dark-skinned boy with dark bushy eyebrows and bright green eyes was sitting on the bed beside him. "If you want, I can show you where to put those special things," he said.

Gavriel was surprised. He wondered how this boy knew about his important things. Noticing the look on Gavriel's face, the boy smiled at him, revealing two large dimples.

"Everyone here has a few treasures from home. Later, if you want, I can show you a good spot for them. And, by the way, I am Yona, Yona Franco, and I am eleven years old."

Gavriel smiled in return and was just about to say something when he was interrupted by a persistent banging sound coming from the corridor. Startled, Gavriel asked Yona, "What's that noise?"

"That's the sign that it's time for us to return to school." All of the boys started to run out of the room. Yona stood up.

"Come on, you don't want to be late on your first day. Follow me, I'll show you where to go." Yona ran out of the room, with Gavriel quickly following behind him.

Meanwhile, Mrs. Habib was walking home, having just mailed her letter to Perla and Gedalia Perahia. Mrs. Habib, whose eyesight was failing and whose hands were shaky with age, had addressed the letter to 111, Earls Lane, Leeds, England, and not 11, Earlscourt Lane, Leeds, England.

The letter would never reach Gavriel's aunt and uncle.

**CHAPTER NINE**

Daniel arrived home one morning to find a long brown envelope addressed to him with the words "On His Majesty's Service" emblazoned on the front. Daniel knew exactly what this was; since the advent of conscription, the joke had been that an envelope bearing such marking contained one's "personal invitation from the king" – instructions from the British Army about where and when to report for basic training.

After speaking with the other boys in the neighborhood who had enlisted with him, Daniel realized that the recruiting sergeant, Sergeant Connor, had indeed managed to have all twelve of them sent to the same place for basic training. They had all received letters instructing them to report to the military barracks at the Tower of London, the ancient fortress that stood on the north bank of the Thames River, on September 25, 1916, at 9 a.m. in the morning.

During the weeks before they were scheduled to report to the barracks, Daniel and his three friends talked of little else every time they saw each other. They knew that basic training could last anywhere from four to twelve weeks, and that there was the possibility that they could then be shipped out and sent overseas to fight.

The night before they were to report to the Tower, the friends sat and talked in the Goldblooms' front room. Characteristically, Moishe was not concerned about what awaited them. "Everything is fine. We are all together and based in the city, which means that we can probably go home sometimes for *Shabbos*. We will be able to get kosher food, and we will have a *minyan*. There is nothing to worry about."

Chezki agreed with Moishe. "Yes, Moishe, it looks like your father's plan is working out. But you know, anything can happen. The army can do whatever it wants, whenever it wants. We could report to the Tower and then we could be told that some of us are being sent to basic training somewhere completely different, maybe Wales, for all we know."

Avrumi nodded in agreement with Chezki, which was a rare occurrence. The two of them had spent years disagreeing with each other; it was the cornerstone of their friendship. "As much as it pains me to say this, in this instance, I think Chezki is right. What the army decides today and what could be in store for us in a few weeks' time could be two very different things."

Daniel considered this possibility. "You may be right, but right now, *Baruch Hashem*, for the time being, we are all together. We have to be appreciative of that. We can't worry now about what the future might bring."

"Daniel, Daniel, always the voice of reason and common sense," Chezki joked, but of course, he and the other boys knew that Daniel was right.

The next morning it was time for Daniel to say good-bye to his parents and his sisters. His father had wanted to accompany Daniel to the Tower, but Daniel had insisted that there was no need, that he would be fine and that all of the boys were going to go together. "Daniel," his father kept asking, "are you sure you don't want me to come with you?"

"No, Papa, you need your sleep. Before you know it, it will be time to start baking again for tomorrow," said Daniel.

Daniel's mother said very little. Esthereva was a reserved woman who kept her thoughts and feelings to herself. She had prepared a small bag of food for Daniel, and as she handed it to him she simply said, "Take good care of yourself."

Henia, the oldest of Daniel's sisters, was fifteen and she was the most emotional and sensitive of the three. Every time she looked at her brother, she burst into tears. "Henia, I am not even leaving the city," Daniel reassured her. "I am just going a few blocks away."

Yetta, Daniel's middle sister, was twelve. She had a very warm, outgoing personality. All the customers in the bakery liked her; she usually remembered their names and she always had something pleasant to say. "Daniel, we are going to miss you so much! Please try to come home for *Shabbos*, every *Shabbos*. Ask them; tell them it is important to us that you are here."

Daniel looked at her and in a sincere voice he said, "Yetta,

I will try. I will try very hard to come home, but you know that it is not going to be up to me. It will be up to the army to decide."

Finally, Daniel's youngest sister Devora, who was eight, looked up at Daniel. "You can't go, you can't go. Who am I going to talk to?"

Daniel looked at her and laughed. "Devora, you have Mama and Papa and your two big sisters to talk to, and your friends and Tante Faiga, and all the customers in the shop. You have lots of people to talk to."

"But Daniel, they don't talk to me like you do. You talk to me and you actually listen to me, too."

Daniel smiled at her. "Don't worry, with *Hashem*'s help I will be home soon, and then I will listen to everything that you have to say."

At that moment, Moishe appeared in the Sheinfelds' front hall. After saying hello to Daniel's parents he said, "Daniel, we need to go. Reb Blau and Chezki are already downstairs waiting for us." Daniel gave everyone in his family a quick hug and then followed Moishe down the stairs.

The twelve boys from the neighborhood reached the Tower of London in less than an hour. When Daniel first caught sight of the imposing, enormous stone tower, he remembered his father telling him how he and Daniel's mother had docked at Irongate Stairs, right near the Tower Bridge, when they first arrived in England.

Though Daniel was not overly pensive by nature, he could not help but wonder for a brief moment how his parents would have felt all those years ago if they had known then that some seventeen years later, their infant son would return to this very spot as a British soldier.

A number of other boys had already gathered at the Tower. Soon, they were met by a tall dark-haired soldier who introduced himself as Corporal Reynolds. He informed the group that he had been given the task of processing them and handing out their uniforms and supplies.

After checking their names against his list, Corporal Reynolds formed them up and called them to attention.

"Each of you has the rank of a 'private.' You will be referred to by your last name. You are to call everyone in the army who has a more senior rank than you by his rank only, and *never* by his last name. You will refer to me as Corporal, and to Sergeant Pape, who you will soon meet, as Sergeant."

As they walked down the long corridor, Reynolds continued to instruct the new soldiers. "You will stand at attention and initiate the salute each and every time an officer talks to you. When an officer is finished talking to you, he will dismiss you, and there will be another exchange of salutes. Remember, you must always salute an officer, and you must always initiate the salute."

Reynolds continued. "Rank is indicated by the number of yellow chevrons that are sewn on the right sleeve of the uniform. The chevron is in the shape of a yellow triangle, pointed upwards. You new recruits do not have a chevron. Corporals, such as myself, have two chevrons," he said, pointing proudly to his upper sleeve, "and sergeants have three, theirs being khaki in color. Pay attention to rank. Do not make a mistake."

"You have been assigned to the $60^{th}$ $2^{nd}/2^{nd}$ London Division. You will now get your uniforms. The insignia of the London Division is the bumblebee. It is stitched to the upper sleeves of the shirt, and the words '$60^{th}$ $2^{nd}/2^{nd}$ London Division' are sewn above in an arc. The division's insignia is also on your cap."

Corporal Reynolds stopped in front of a large wooden door and knocked loudly. A soldier, who looked almost as young as Daniel and his friends, opened the door, revealing a large room filled with hundreds and hundreds of identical uniforms, peaked caps and boots.

"Get out of your civvies and wait in line. Smythe will get you kitted out. You have ten minutes." Corporal Reynolds turned briskly on his heel and walked away.

"Civvies," whispered Chezki to his friends, noticing their confusion. "'Civvies' means civilian clothes. This soldier named Smythe must be a private like us, and he will give each of us a uniform."

One by one, each boy was fitted with an army regulation tunic and shirt. The shirt had metal buttons, two breast pockets with pleats, two side pockets with flaps, and a turned-down collar. They were then given pants made of the same fabric, and woolen puttees, bandage-like cloths that were meant to be wound around the lower legs. Each new soldier was also issued a pair of plain ankle boots called "ammunition boots," woolen socks, a greatcoat and a woolen cap, all of them the same greenish khaki color.

Corporal Reynolds soon returned and led the boys down the hall to another large room. Here, each soldier was given a haversack that contained a tin plate, a small teapot and lid, a tea strainer, a condiment can, an alcohol burner with lid and stand, a bottle of water, a blanket, basic first aid supplies and a waterproof cape. Each soldier was also given a kitbag containing personal items, such as brushes, soap and an extra blanket. A complete change of clothing and extra boots would be added to the kitbag later.

Once everyone had been assigned a haversack and a kitbag, Colonel Reynolds announced, "And now, for my favorite part of orientation, a trip to the barber!" All of the new soldiers were soon issued an extremely short army regulation haircut. The twelve Jewish soldiers from the East End asked the barber to please make sure to leave untouched the corners of their hair at the sides of their heads.

They were then shown an enormous room that was lined from wall to wall with beds, a number of which were bare. A pillow, a sheet and a blanket were piled together at the foot of each bed. "Find an available bed and make it, and I will be back in ten minutes," instructed the corporal.

Moishe soon spotted a number of empty beds beside each other at the far corner of the room. "Come on, let's get those four together," he told his friends. He immediately went over to the corner and started to make one of the beds. The other boys quickly followed. As they made the beds, they teased each other about their new haircuts, trying to decide who looked the funniest. They decided that it had to be Chezki; with his mass of curly brown hair now gone, he looked like a newly shorn sheep.

Corporal Reynolds returned, telling the soldiers that it was time for lunch. He led them into the dining room. Long wooden tables were set up in rows and there was a long counter at one end, behind which stood a number of men. These men were serving the soldiers, ladling out portions of food. "Form up," Corporal Reynolds instructed. "You have half an hour. Be ready to leave at 1:00 p.m. for drill training with Sergeant Pape. And I do mean half an hour. Don't be late."

As all of the other soldiers started to line up to get their food, the twelve boys from the East End stood and looked at each other, unsure of what to do. They had been told that the rabbi on the home front, Chaplain Lipson, had secured provisions for kosher food for the Jewish soldiers undergoing basic training. Was this kept in a separate room? Who should they talk to?

Chezki decided that the simplest thing to do was to ask one of the soldiers standing behind the counter. In his typical outgoing manner, he approached one of them.

"Hello there, we are new here and ..."

"New here? Why, you don't say?" interjected the soldier, in mock surprise.

Chezki continued. "Today is our first day at the barracks, and there are twelve of us who require special food, special kosher food."

Again the soldier interjected, "Special kosher food, is that a fact? And what would '*ko-shure*' food be, exactly?"

"It is food that has been prepared according to the Jewish dietary laws, and I believe that Chaplain Lipson has made arrangements for –"

The soldier cut him off again. "Really, specially prepared food. I would like some of that myself, maybe a nice piece of beef, Yorkshire pudding and some spuds. Yes, I certainly have missed specially prepared food …."

From his seat at the far side of the room, an older, tired-looking soldier noticed that a number of the new soldiers were milling around and had not yet started to eat. He approached the group, his irritation clearly visible on his face.

"I am Sergeant Pape," he said. "What is going on here? This is not a fancy restaurant. This is the army. Go get your food and sit down. What are you waiting for?"

Chezki, feeling a little flummoxed by now, did not answer.

Avrumi stepped forward. "Sergeant, we are of the Jewish faith and our religion does not allow us to eat the regular army food. We are under the impression that there has been an arrangement made for Jewish soldiers, an arrangement made with Chaplain Lipson of the Home Office, for the provision of kosher food. We are not sure where to get it."

"Oh, the special Jewish food," said Sergeant Pape, with a hint of annoyance in his voice. Looking closely at the boys' faces and at the yarmulkes that were peeking out from their newly issued caps, he said irritably, to no one in particular, "I might have guessed."

Turning to the soldier behind the counter he said, "Roberts, what are you playing at? You know about the Jewish food. Go and get it immediately."

"Yes, Sergeant," replied the soldier.

"Your special food is on its way," the sergeant said to the boys. He stood there and glared at the boys for a minute, and then he suddenly walked away.

Feeling acutely ill at ease, Daniel and the others stood and waited at the counter until the food appeared. By then, it was almost one o'clock. The boys washed, ate and *bentched* as quickly as possible, all the while feeling the cold hard eyes of Sergeant Pape on them from across the room.

**G**avriel had been at the orphanage for almost a month. Yona had befriended him immediately, and he had been happy to show Gavriel around and explain the routine. The two boys soon told each other about their families.

Yona was the only child of elderly parents, both of whom had died many years ago, within months of each other. Yona had been placed in the Allatini Orphanage when he was just five years old, and he remembered almost nothing of his parents, Mathilde and Salomon Franco. He had a photograph of them, and one afternoon, he showed it to Gavriel. Gavriel, in turn, showed Yona the photograph of him and his mother, taken more than two years ago when Gavriel had turned nine.

Gavriel also showed Yona his kaleidoscope, a gift his aunt and uncle had sent him a few years earlier. Gavriel loved the kaleidoscope, and he had spent many hours using it, both inside the Benvenistes' house and outside in the *cortijo*. Sometimes he even used it while walking down the street; his mother used to joke that Gavriel was so engrossed by it that one day he was likely to get lost and suddenly find himself in Athens.

After a short time, Gavriel made friends with a number of the other boys, and almost all of them soon came to appreciate Gavriel's positive outlook and happy disposition.

Despite his relatively easy adjustment to life in the orphanage, Gavriel spent most of his waking hours thinking about joining his aunt and uncle in England. He was starting to grow slightly impatient.

Mr. Capon had not said a word to him about England, and Gavriel had begun to worry that maybe the director of the orphanage had forgotten. One afternoon when the boys had free time, Gavriel decided to speak to him. After all, hadn't his mother always said, "*Quien duerme, no alcansa pexe* (One who sleeps catches no fish)."

The dark wooden door to Mr. Capon's office was closed. Gavriel knew by now this meant that Mr. Capon was meeting with someone about accepting a new boy in the orphanage. Gavriel realized he might have a long wait, but he did not want to weaken his resolve by returning to his room. As he stood in the hall thinking about the adjustment a new boy would have to make, he thought about his first meal in the orphanage all those weeks ago.

At dinner time, Sebi had taken a seat right beside Gavriel. As the boys began to eat, he had said to Gavriel, "You see the *fijones* on your plate? Can I have it? I am really very hungry today. I don't know why."

Gavriel, not realizing that the boys were only allowed one

portion of each item, said, "Yes, I guess so. If you are really hungry, you can have it." Sebi took the *fijones* and stuffed them into his mouth, making noisy, exaggerated sounds as he chewed.

Then, eyeing Gavriel's plate again, he said, "That *calavasicas* of yours looks very tasty, too. Do you mind if I try it?"

"Well, you could have a bit –" Without waiting for Gavriel to finish, Sebi scooped it up with his fork and stuck it in his mouth. When he was finished, he belched loudly, and then reached over in a quick motion and grabbed the two pieces of bread that were on Gavriel's plate.

He tore into the bread, and with his mouth full he said, "Delicious. There is nothing like fresh bread to go with a meal."

As Gavriel looked around, he saw a lot of the boys staring at him, to see how he was going to react.

Yona whispered to Gavriel, "There are no seconds. Sebi has taken your entire dinner." Gavriel felt as though he had been stung. He had been trying to be nice, and Sebi had been making a fool of him. And in addition to that, he now had no dinner.

In an effort to sound as reasonable as possible, he said, "Sebi, I am sorry, but I didn't realize that we were not allowed any more food. Now that you have taken all of mine, I do not have anything left to eat for dinner."

Sebi looked at Gavriel and laughed. "Nothing left to eat? Nothing? How sad! A growing boy like you, without any food. I know what we'll do! We'll call the cook. Yes, a special cook will come and prepare a fancy meal for the very important Gavriel." Sebi was being his usual self, showing off, trying to sound important. He could not have known how deeply these words hurt Gavriel.

Gavriel's mother Allegra had been a cook, and when she would prepare fancy meals or special foods for her employers, she would always save him something, telling Gavriel that because he was so important, a special cook had been hired just to make meals for him.

Sebi continued to taunt Gavriel. "Don't you have anything to say for yourself, Gavriel? Or are you too weak from hunger to talk?" Sebi started laughing loudly, and a number of other boys joined in.

Gavriel, trying to sound confident, said calmly, "Its fine, Sebi. I know that it is a *mitzvah* to share, and I realize now that you were very hungry. Thank you for letting me perform this *mitzvah*."

Sebi looked surprised. Clearly, it was not the response he had hoped for. Tears and pleading usually followed his taunts, but Gavriel's response was so reasoned, so mature. Sebi wiped his mouth with the back of his hand and muttered, "I'll speak to you later." Then he angrily stomped away.

The boys at the table began to talk amongst themselves. Had Gavriel outsmarted Sebi? Sebi never walked away from anything. They were shocked at how this new boy had stood up to him. Shocked, but also impressed.

One of the boys said to Gavriel with a smile, "That was so clever. You actually made Sebi feel that he did you a favor."

Another boy tapped Gavriel on the shoulder and said, "That was smart. I liked the way you did that." In a few minutes' time, a number of boys had started talking to Gavriel and had introduced themselves.

Eventually, Gavriel found out from Yona that Sebi was the oldest boy at the orphanage, and that he had been there the longest. The story that circulated in the boys' room, though no one knew if it was true or not, was that Sebi had been left in the care of the orphanage by his mother, who had told Mr. Capon that she needed someone to watch her young son just for an afternoon. That had been nine years ago, and she had not been seen since.

Sebi was adept at pretending to be a well-mannered and polite boy in front of adults, but in reality he was a nasty, aggressive bully. He behaved as though the room in the orphanage was exclusively his, and he viewed all the other boys as his servants. Through the threat of force, he had "convinced" one boy to make his bed, one boy to clean his shoes and one boy to hand over his dinner. If any of the boys complained and said that they were going to tell Mr. Capon, Sebi would simply smirk and say, "Who is Mr. Capon going to believe, me or you? He has known me since I was a little boy, and he trusts me completely."

Gavriel soon learned to keep his distance from Sebi. Sebi would occasionally taunt Gavriel and say, "Hey, I hear a boat is leaving for England tomorrow," but, generally, Sebi left him alone. Sebi, though he did not want to admit this to himself, was reluctant to confront Gavriel. He knew that Gavriel was very clever and that any verbal altercation between the two would end with Sebi losing. Sebi had more fun teasing boys whom he could make cry, and then boss around.

The door to Mr. Capon's office finally opened, interrupting Gavriel's thoughts. As the director ushered out a distraught-looking young woman, he noticed Gavriel waiting for him in the hall. His face registered surprise; Gavriel had never come to speak to him before. Although there were boys who were always showing up at his office to complain about this or ask for that, Gavriel was certainly not one of them. In the weeks Gavriel had been here, he had been a model of good behavior.

"Gavriel, my boy, are you waiting to speak to me?" Gavriel nodded. Mr. Capon continued, "Gavriel, I will return in a minute. I must escort this young woman to the door. Please wait for me inside my office." Gavriel went inside and sat down on one of the narrow wooden chairs.

In a few minutes, Mr. Capon returned and quickly took a seat behind his desk as he smiled at Gavriel.

"Tell me, Gavriel, why have you come to see me?" Gavriel felt momentarily awkward and did not quite know how to begin. He began slowly.

"Mr. Capon, I have been here almost a month and I was wondering … well, you see, I was thinking perhaps now is a good time to send me to England. I know there is still a war going on, but maybe it has become safer for me to travel. After all, I am certain my aunt and uncle are waiting for me, and are expecting me to come very soon."

Gavriel paused and looked at the director hopefully. Mr. Capon looked at the boy compassionately. He had heard this reasoning many times before – a child clinging to the hope that someone, somewhere, still wanted him, still cared about him.

Sighing deeply, Mr. Capon said to Gavriel, "Yes, I am sure that you are looking forward to being reunited with your aunt and uncle. Unfortunately, there is still a ban on travel at the moment. I cannot possibly allow you to even think of leaving at the moment."

Noticing the boy's disappointment, Mr. Capon quickly thought of something he believed might console him. "However, Gavriel, I think I have an idea that you might like. I know that on *Shabbat* you have been going to the synagogue at the Talmud Torah with all the other boys." He paused, and Gavriel nodded. "I know also that your family is of Italian origin, and that you used to go to the *Italia Yashan*, the synagogue of Italian immigrants. Well, would you like to go there on *Shabbat*? I think we could trust you to get there on your own. Perhaps you might see some familiar faces, some old friends of yours? And," Mr. Capon added, "I think that your new friend, Yona Franco, might like to go with you. I seem to remember his parents were of Italian origin, as well. He would probably enjoy the familiar customs and language."

Gavriel's face brightened at the thought. He would dearly love to return to the *Italia Yashan*, the synagogue where he and his mother had gone every *Shabbat* morning for years.

And he was certain Yona would enjoy it, as well. Yona knew very little about his own background, and this way, Gavriel could teach him a few things. 'Mr. Capon, I would love to go. Thank you so much. Can I tell Yona?"

"Certainly," the director replied, pleased that he had been able to think of something to cheer up the disappointed boy. "It is time to return to school now, Gavriel. Now go and join the other boys," instructed Mr. Capon. Gavriel stood up at once, anxious to find Yona and tell him the news. True, he hadn't achieved what he had come for, but he was very happy to be able to return to the *Italia Yashan*. He thanked Mr. Capon a second time and quickly left the office.

As Mr. Capon watched Gavriel leave, his heart lurched. The boy was bound to find out the truth sooner or later, but how long could Mr. Capon pretend that his plans for England would actually materialize?

Mr. Capon did not have the heart to tell Gavriel why, despite the fact that civilian travel was indeed a little bit safer at the moment, he had made no plans yet to send him to England. The real reason Gavriel could not go to England was because his aunt and uncle had not responded to Mrs. Habib's letter.

# CHAPTER ELEVEN

*London*
*November 1916*

From the very first day that they had arrived for basic training, Daniel and all the boys from the East End had remained under the constant scrutiny of Sergeant Pape. Pape instructed the new soldiers in all aspects of military life – how to follow regulations and orders, battle drill, field skills, bayonet fighting, musketry, hygiene, digging and marching – endless, endless marching, sometimes covering as much as 100 miles in five days.

The soldiers wore a webbed belt at the waist with two pouches of ammunition suspended from several buckles. They carried a rifle, a bayonet, their haversacks and their kitbags – an extremely heavy load. The marches were very difficult, especially for the soldiers who were not used to physical labor, and many of them struggled to keep up.

Every day, many times a day, Sergeant Pape would repeat, "The main objective of basic training is to toughen you up, to make you into men." Daniel and his friends felt that Sergeant Pape's real objective was to turn all of them into obedient machines who would immediately and automatically, without thinking, follow any order issued by any of their superiors.

One afternoon, after the other soldiers had just completed another long march and were heading back inside the Tower, Sergeant Pape approached Daniel. Daniel was surprised because the sergeant had never approached any of them directly. "Sheinfeld, come here," said the sergeant.

Daniel said, "Yes, Sergeant." He was worried. *Why did the sergeant want to talk to him?*

"I have noticed you marching; you never seem to tire."

"Yes, Sergeant," Daniel replied again, not knowing why this was of interest to the sergeant.

"What did you do before you enlisted?"

"I worked at my father's bakery, mainly as a delivery boy."

"I see. Did you cover far distances on foot?"

"Yes, Sergeant. I covered a three-mile radius twice a day."

"What else did you do at the bakery?" the sergeant asked.

"I was in charge of the telephone during the day. I took telephone orders from the few customers who owned telephones, and I called our suppliers to place orders."

The sergeant looked pleased by what Daniel had told him. "That will be all. Carry on, Sheinfeld."

Daniel quickly joined the rest of his friends who were now standing in the hall. They all started to talk to him at once. "What did the sergeant want?" asked Chezki. "He never talks to us. He just scowls at us occasionally."

"Daniel," said Moishe, echoing Chezki, "why did he want to talk to you? Are you in trouble?" Daniel then recounted the conversation to his friends and admitted to them that he had found the whole thing rather odd.

"I can't think of a single reason why he would care that I worked in a bakery," said Daniel. "And furthermore, why would it matter if I used a telephone?"

Avrumi, who until this point had yet to say anything, now added, "You know, Daniel, the sergeant wasn't just making idle conversation. I think he has something special in mind for you and wanted to know if you have certain skills." Chezki shook his head.

"Oh, come on, Reb Blau! Special skills? Like deciding which customer should get the *brahnbroit* and which customer should get the *lubben*?" All of them started to laugh because the whole encounter seemed so absurd.

Suddenly, Private Smythe approached them. The boys, Chezki in particular, were very friendly with him, and had been since the first few days after they had arrived. Smythe seemed to make it a point to be exceptionally nice to Daniel and his friends. Having been stationed at the Tower of London barracks for almost a year, he understood all the ins and outs of basic training and was happy to explain things to the boys.

Smythe also seemed to know in advance what was happening next and was always willing to share this information. He knew before it was announced when they would be allowed home on leave, what was for dinner and when new recruits would be arriving. He was a very useful person to know.

"Katz, I have news, big news," said Smythe, referring to Chezki by his last name.

"What is it, Smythe? Are we getting leave for this weekend?" asked Chezki.

"No, Katz. I said I have big news, very big news."

"What is it, Smythe? Tell us, don't keep us in suspense."

"I heard that Sergeant Pape is going to be instructing all of you in gas defense today after lunch," said Smythe.

"So, big deal! Another afternoon spent with the sergeant is nothing to get excited about," answered Chezki brashly.

"Katz, don't be a fool. Everyone is always shipped out after they learn gas defense," Smythe said with certainty.

Chezki paused for a minute. He had to admit to himself that for the past two months, Smythe had been a very reliable source of information and had never once been wrong. "Really? When?" asked Chezki, his voice wavering slightly.

"Oh, I am guessing they'll let you have a few days' leave and then ship you out by the end of the week. Listen, I'm sorry, I have to go now. Corporal Reynolds is waiting for me. I'll talk to you later." And with that, Smythe was gone.

As they headed toward the dining room, Daniel and his friends discussed Smythe's news. They sat down in what had become their regular spot in the room and told the other eight boys from the East End what they had just heard. Some of the other boys claimed to already have heard that they were about to be shipped out, while others dismissed it as a baseless rumor.

Engrossed as they were in discussion, they did not notice Sergeant Pape enter the room. He came over to their table and instructed them, "You are expected in the assembly room in ten minutes. Finish your grub immediately, and don't dawdle over that song you always sing after meals. Don't be late."

"This is it," Chezki said as soon as the sergeant turned his back and began to walk away. "We are going to be instructed in gas warfare. Smythe was right, I am sure of it."

As they walked into the room, they immediately saw that Smythe was correct. Gas masks were lying on the floor, lined up in rows. The masks consisted of a brown rubberized face piece with a thin red rubber exhaust valve attached at the back. The equipment included a box respirator, to be worn on the chest in the case of poison gas attacks, and a carrier for the mask.

Moishe was scared. He whispered anxiously to Avrumi, "Oh, this is exactly what Smythe said. We are learning gas defense! This means we are being shipped out!"

"Moishe," said Avrumi in a low voice, "we don't know this for a fact. You must be quiet or you won't hear what the sergeant is saying and understand what he is talking about."

Sergeant Pape began. "This afternoon, I am going to teach all of you the proper procedure in the event of a gas attack. Now pay close attention. The Huns (Germans) have been using gas since 1915. You lot need to understand how to protect yourselves in the event of a gas attack."

For the next hour, the soldiers practiced putting on and taking off the gas masks. They practiced helping their fellow soldiers secure theirs, and they learned how to reattach the box to the tubing if it became detached.

Once the practice was over, Sergeant Pape announced, "You're being shipped out. You have a 24-hour leave beginning at 22:00. You will march to Victoria Station Thursday morning and will board a train to Southampton. Say goodbye to your family on Wednesday. Under no circumstances will they be allowed to accompany you on Thursday. If they are so inclined, they may line the streets along the way and watch you depart from a distance. Dismissed."

Sergeant Pape quickly left the room to avoid the many questions that inevitably followed these announcements.

Chezki, without the usual bravado he normally used when he was proven right, said softly, "Smythe knew. He knew. This is exactly what he predicted."

Moishe, his cheeks flushed and his brow wet with sweat, kept shaking his head. "I can't believe it, we're going to be shipped out, I can't believe it."

Avrumi, a shocked look on his face, said with incredulity, "Me, they are sending me overseas to fight? I can't fight. This can't be, this just can't be."

Daniel remained silent. All he could think of was his parents, his poor mother and father. How could he possibly tell them that he, Daniel, their only son, the son who had been born to them after such incredible suffering, was being sent overseas to fight on the blood-soaked battlefields of France?

*Salonika*
*November 1916*

# CHAPTER TWELVE

The *Shabbat* following his conversation with Mr. Capon, Gavriel and Yona went to the *Italia Yashan* synagogue. The congregation, which was also called the *Kehilla Kedosha Italia*, had been established in 1423 by immigrants from Sicily. Later, in the sixteenth century, an influx of Italian refugees had joined the congregation, and it was one of the oldest and most established synagogues in Salonika.

Gavriel proudly led Yona into the synagogue. Gavriel's mother had taken Gavriel here ever since he had been old enough to walk, and since her death two years ago, he had come here numerous times on his own. Yona, who had never been there before, was wide-eyed as he surveyed the beautiful synagogue. He gazed with awe at the magnificently carved marble arch and pillars that encased the intricately decorated double doors of the *Aron Kodesh*. He stared at the elaborately upholstered chairs that flanked the *Aron* on either side, and when Yona looked up, he saw the enormous *ner tamid* suspended from the ceiling. He marveled at the exquisitely crafted, elevated *bima,* adorned with a number of stately candelabra.

Upon taking his seat, Gavriel immediately saw a number of familiar faces among the congregants. Many of the men and boys recognized him and smiled in his direction. Most of them had heard that the Benveniste family had moved and that Gavriel was now living at the Allatini Orphanage. They looked at him now, happily pointing things out to an unfamiliar boy, and he still seemed to possess his usual cheerful disposition. After *Mussaf,* the men approached him, warmly shaking his hand and that of his friend and wishing them a *"Shabbat Shalom."*

Once everyone had departed the building, Gavriel said to Yona, "Come upstairs. I want to show you something."

"Upstairs, you mean in the women's section? What's upstairs?" asked Yona.

"Follow me. Come on and you'll see," said Gavriel, a mysterious smile on his face.

The two boys ascended the creaky wooden staircase. When they reached the top, Gavriel opened the small door leading to the women's section and went inside. Yona followed, still not understanding what Gavriel wanted to show him. "Oh, did you want to show me the view, from up here?" asked Yona.

"No, Yona, we aren't looking at the view. I want to show you something special here, at the side."

Gavriel walked over to the right-hand corner of the women's section and motioned for Yona to follow. Yona obliged, and both boys soon came to a small unpainted wooden door. The door frame was so low it was hard to imagine anyone being able to get inside.

A distinctly musty smell emanated from the room as Gavriel slowly opened the door. The room was no bigger than an alcove, full of stacks of ancient books and boxes overflowing with papers, curled and yellowed with age. Ducking his head, Gavriel stepped inside, and Yona crammed in closely behind him.

"This was my special hiding place for years when I was a little boy," Gavriel said. "You see, my mother brought me to this synagogue every week. She would always sit in the same place – fourth row, fifth seat. And every week I would sit in the seat beside her, on her right. She would pay close attention to the words in her *siddur*, never once interrupting her prayers to talk to me, or anyone else for that matter. For the first little while I would sit quietly with my mother, but then I would start to fidget. Soon, I would get restless, and I would stand up. In no time, I would be walking around. You know, I remember, all the women in the surrounding seats were so nice to me. They never scolded me for moving around; I think they understood that I did not have a father to sit with in the synagogue and I had nowhere else to go.

"One day, when I was maybe around five or so, as I walked around, I happened to notice a small door. I was curious, so I went over to the door, carefully turned the handle and slowly pulled. To my delight, the door opened – I had discovered this little room. I realized immediately that it was the perfect hiding spot for me, that amidst all of the books and the papers there was just enough room for me to sit down. And so, from that day onwards, I would go into 'my' special room whenever I grew restless. I would look at the old books, rummage through the crumbling papers and sometimes just sit and daydream. My mother eventually found out about the little room, but she didn't seem to mind. Every *Shabbat* after *Mussaf*, when it was time to leave, she would come to the front of the little door and quietly say, 'Gavriel, it is time to go now. Come along. It's not polite to keep everyone at home waiting.'"

Gavriel paused for a moment, almost as if lost in the memory. Then he resumed. "After my mother died, I continued to come to *shul*, but of course, I now sat in the men's section. After all, I was now almost eleven years old and had no reason to be in the women's section anymore. But sometimes after *Mussaf*, I would come up here, just for a few minutes, and sit in this little room. It reminded me of my mother and made me feel somehow closer to her.

"Then of course, once I went to live at the orphanage, I could no longer come here on *Shabbat*, and I went with all the other boys to the big synagogue at the *Talmud Torah*. When Mr. Capon gave me permission to come back here I was thrilled. I had missed the *Italia Yashan* and, I have to admit, I missed this little room. I didn't tell Mr. Capon about it, and I have never told anyone else about it either. But since I showed you the whole synagogue today, I felt that I wanted to show you this room, too."

Yona looked at Gavriel. "Gavriel, thank you for telling me

about the room, and thank you for bringing me here today. I'm so lucky to have you as a friend."

Everyone at the orphanage knew that Gavriel was a very special person, not just because he was clever and good-hearted, but also because Gavriel had something wonderful – a seemingly unshakeable *emunah*, a firm belief that *Senor del Mundo* was guiding the world. Gavriel believed that every-thing was part of His plan and that, somehow, everything was for the best.

Gavriel smiled at Yona. "Well, hopefully, Mr. Capon will let us keep coming here on *Shabbat*, especially when he hears how much you like being here. But you know, if we are late for lunch, he for sure won't let us return, so we better hurry back. Come on. Let's go, let's go. I'll race you!!"

The two boys quickly left the room, scrambled down the stairs, swung open the large front door and ran out of the building. On their way back to the orphanage, they saw many other Jewish people heading back to their homes for lunch. As they passed, they all nodded and wished each other a "*Shabbat Shalom.*"

Right before they reached the orphanage, they noticed a few soldiers walking along the street. This was not an uncom-mon site; many soldiers were stationed near Salonika, and when they were given leave they often came into the city. As the boys drew closer, Gavriel thought he detected the sounds of people speaking English.

"Yona, slow down for a second. I want to hear what these soldiers are saying," he said to his friend.

"Sure, Gavriel, if you want to," said Yona, who knew that his friend understood English. The boys stood near the soldiers, and Gavriel tried, as unobtrusively as possible, to hear what they were talking about.

"So then Atwood says to me, 'There is a civilian ship bound for England disembarking from the port of Salonika in a fortnight.' And then I say to him, 'Really, I never hear anything, the sergeant keeps me so busy ....'"

The soldier, suddenly aware of Gavriel's and Yona's presence, stopped talking mid-sentence. He turned around abruptly and glared at the boys. Gavriel and Yona clearly understood the soldier's unspoken message. Embarrassed, they quickly walked away.

"Yona, Yona, I understood what the soldier said!" Gavriel exclaimed excitedly as they continued walking toward the orphanage. "A ship is going back to England soon – in a 'fortnight' – whatever that means. He said it was a ship of civilians, not army people! That means they could take me! I could go on that ship, too. I just need to find out more about it. Yona, this is wonderful! I know exactly what I'll do. I'll find out all about it, and then I will give Mr. Capon all the details. I know he is so busy, always in meetings. But I am sure that I could arrange almost all of it myself, and then there will be no reason not to send me. After all, he knows that I am only staying at the orphanage for a short time, that my aunt and uncle are expecting me." Gavriel had a huge smile on his face.

"How are you going to find out more about the ship? You

saw how the soldiers reacted; they certainly don't want boys hanging around, eavesdropping on their conversations."

"You are right, Yona. I am not sure. I will need to think of something, but I am certain there is a way," replied Gavriel.

By now the boys had reached the front door of the orphanage. As they went inside, they could see that all the boys were already heading toward the dining room. "We better hurry up; we don't want to miss *Kiddush*," said Yona. Gavriel followed, anxiously anticipating the free time he would have later in the day to think about what he had just heard from the British soldiers.

# CHAPTER THIRTEEN

*London*
*November 1916*

It was almost 11 p.m., and Daniel knew that he would find his father in the bakery. Without stopping first to say hello to his mother, he went in through the back door of the building and quietly headed downstairs.

His father was seated at a small table. A large glass jar and several flats of eggs were in front of him. He was busy cracking eggs and checking for blood spots, and he did not notice Daniel come in.

"Hello, Papa, I am home," Daniel announced, trying to keep his voice steady. At the sound of his son's voice, his father stood up and quickly came over to embrace him.

"Daniel, Daniel, *shalom aleichem*, it is so good to see you!" he enthused. "How are you? Have you said hello to Mama yet?"

"*Aleichem shalom*, Papa. I am fine, and no, I have not seen Mama yet. I have just now walked home from the barracks; we were given a 24-hour leave. I came straight away to the bakery. I wanted to talk to you first." He paused for a moment, unsure of what exactly to say. "What I mean is that ... I have something important that I need to tell you ....”

“I see,” his father said quietly. “What is it that you want to tell me?”

“Papa,” answered Daniel softly, “perhaps you would like to sit down again.”

His father drew a quick breath. “No, Daniel, I will remain standing. Tell me whatever it is that needs to be told.”

Daniel looked at his father. He could tell from the look on his face that his father already knew what Daniel was about to say. Yet, Daniel knew that he actually had to say the words out loud, that somehow this would make it more believable for both him and for his father.

“Papa,” Daniel said hesitantly, “I am being shipped out this Thursday morning. Me, Moishe, Chezki and Avrumi, all twelve of us from here who enlisted together, as well as many other boys in our division.”

“I see,” said his father for the second time. “Do you know where you are being sent?”

“I am not sure, Papa. Everyone assumes it will be somewhere in France, on the Western Front.”

His face now completely drained of color, his father sat back down at the small table. With his head in his hands, he slowly said to himself, over and over again, “The Western Front ... the Western Front ...”

Finally, looking up at his son, Mottel instructed, “Daniel, you are not to tell your mother about this now. Allow her the pleasure of having you home for the night. Go upstairs, have a cup of tea together, let her make you something to eat. Later, later, I will tell her. Tomorrow morning, after your mother knows, you may tell your sisters." His father added, more to himself than to Daniel, "Please, *Hashem*, I only hope that the girls are too young to understand fully what this means."

Almost as if hurrying him out of the room, Mottel waved a large hand in his son's direction. "Go, Daniel, go upstairs now. Go see your mama. She will be so happy to see you."

Mottel pointed to the flats of eggs piled high on the table. "I must return to my work."

"Of course, Papa, I understand. I will go upstairs right away," said Daniel.

As Daniel started up the stairs, he could hear his father cracking eggs against the glass jar and crying, "Esthereva … Esthereva … the Western Front …"

It was clear from his mother's demeanor the next morning that his father had informed her of the news. Although she did not say anything, her eyes revealed a new, intense sadness, and she was even more taciturn than usual.

Daniel knew that he had to tell his sisters that he was being shipped out. After all of the breakfast plates had been cleared and the table wiped, he said, "Girls, I have some news, some news from the army." Yetta, his middle sister, asked hopefully, "Are they letting you leave? Have they decided that they don't need you anymore?"

"No, Yetta, they are not letting me leave. They have decided that they would like me and my friends to go to France for a little while."

"Go to France!" Henia, the oldest, nearly shrieked. "How can they send you to France? It is dangerous in France!"

"Settle yourself, Henia," implored their mother.

Daniel continued. "I am going to be leaving early tomorrow morning. Sergeant Pape told us that if you would like to, you may come and watch us march to the train station. Mama, do you think you and the girls could come and see me off?"

His mother hesitated and then said, "Daniel, is this what you want?"

"Yes, Mama," he answered. "I would like that very much, if it is possible."

"Fine, Daniel, we will be there, and your father, too. We will stand on Leadenhall Street. I have heard that many soldiers march westward on this street."

Abruptly changing the subject, his mother instructed, "Henia, go get ready to open the bakery. And Yetta, Devora, come with me and I will fix your hair. It is almost time to leave for school." Yetta and Henia quickly obliged. Only Devora remained, still seated at her spot at the table.

Daniel's youngest sister had not, as yet, said anything in response to what Daniel had told them. Daniel now looked at her. "Devora, you haven't said a word. Did you hear what I was telling Yetta and Henia? I am going away to France for a little while, with some of my friends."

Devora looked across the table at her brother. "Daniel, you

must be a very important soldier in the army if they need you all the way over in France."

"Well, I wouldn't say that, Devora," replied Daniel, almost smiling. "The army sends lots and lots of young men to France. I am really not that special."

"Oh, Daniel, of course you are special. You are my big brother, my only brother. Oh no, how can you go so far away?" Devora said, her big blue eyes filling with tears.

Daniel stood up from his seat and went over to Devora. He bent down beside her and took her small hands in his. "Devora, we will be farther apart, it is true, but I will always carry you with me."

"How will you carry me with you? I don't understand. I'll be here in our house, in London, and you will be in France somewhere, very far away."

Devora stared intently at her brother. He knew she was waiting for an answer. Daniel knew that he had to think of something to tell her, to reassure her that despite the distance, their special bond would remain unchanged. But what more could he tell her? Suddenly, he realized something. He gently took her hand and put it directly on top of the insignia of his division that was sewn onto his right sleeve.

"Look," he said. "This is the design of my group of soldiers, the group that I belong to. I don't think I ever showed this to you before. Do you see what it is?"

"Yes, Daniel, I do! It is a bumblebee." Slowly, a small smile appeared on Devora's face. "You have a bee on your sleeve, a bee, a *devora* – and I am a bee! I remember you told me this once, years ago, when I was feeling left out because Henia and Yetta didn't want to play with me. You told me how special I was because my name meant 'bee' in Hebrew, and that bees were so important because they make honey and everyone loves honey."

"Exactly," Daniel said, realizing that this idea lifted his little sister's spirits. "Now do you understand how I will be carrying you with me all the time? You are on my uniform. This means that, in a way, you and I will still be together, even when I go to France. And who knows," Daniel continued with a little smile on his face, "maybe you will help me do something important over there."

"Do something important? You think I could help you do something important, you mean, in France?" Devora asked, excited by the prospect of helping her brother.

"Yes, it could happen. You never know," he replied, smiling his lopsided smile.

"Oh, Daniel," said Devora as she hugged him tightly, "I am going to write you all the time. I am going to send you lots and lots of letters, and I will make sure to keep asking you how I can help, and then as soon as you know what the two of us can do together, you must write me and tell me what to do, how to do this important thing, whatever it will be, this, this –"

"This mission," said Daniel.

"Yes, yes, this mission," Devora repeated proudly.

Their mother re-entered the kitchen. "Devora, it is time to go to school. You can talk to Daniel later when you come home in the afternoon," she instructed. "Yes, Mama, I am going," said Devora with a broad smile on her face. Daniel looked at his youngest sister; she was so happy about what he had just told her. Their mission! How completely implausible!

*Well*, Daniel thought to himself, *I guess the idea of this shared mission managed to cheer her up.* And, as ridiculous as it seemed, Daniel realized it had cheered him up a little bit, as well.

# CHAPTER FOURTEEN

"So here's the plan," Gavriel said to Yona the next day after lunch. "When we finish school today, we will go down to the Via Egnata. There are lots of British soldiers there. I used to see them all the time when I walked home from my old *habra*."

"I'll help you in any way I can," said Yona. "I know how important it is for you to find out about the ship."

Gavriel continued. "A lot of these soldiers frequent the outdoor cafes, sitting outside, reading the newspapers, eating and talking. What we need to do is take a short walk, go up and down the street a little bit and try to determine which soldiers look the most approachable.

"How are we going to do that?" asked Yona.

"Well, it's easy! Suppose one is sitting alone, scowling or with an angry look on his face. He probably would not feel like talking to me. But suppose two soldiers are sitting together, talking and smiling, enjoying some cake. They might be a little friendlier, a little easier to talk to. Once we identify whom to ask, I will approach them, and I will try to find out the details about that civilian ship leaving for England. I am sure that at least one British soldier will know about it. If you remember, the soldier we encountered yesterday said that all of them had heard about the ship. My mistake then, I now realize, was that I tried to find out about the ship by listening in on the soldiers' conversation, and of course, no one likes that. But I think that if I am forthright, one of the soldiers is bound to be willing to help me."

Yona listened to Gavriel's plan. It sounded very well thought out. But then he realized something. "Gavriel, did Mr. Capon give you permission?"

"No, Yona, I did not ask him. I know that as long as we stay here in the old city and don't venture too far to the north or near the mountains, we are allowed to be on our own for an hour or so after school. I don't want to tell him yet about the ship; I want to do this myself. Once I know all the details, I will tell him about it, and he can make the final arrangements."

Gavriel spent the rest of the afternoon at school in restless anticipation. At the end of the day when their *rubi* banged his wooden stick on the bench at the front of the classroom, Gavriel and Yona flew out of the school and hurried along the street in the direction of the Via Egnata.

Gavriel did not realize that Sebi had observed their hasty departure from the school. His curiosity piqued, and his jealousy long ago aroused by the fact that Gavriel had succeeded in making such a close friend in the little time he had been in the orphanage, he decided to follow the boys and see what they were doing.

It didn't take long for Gavriel and Yona to reach the Via Egnata, and just as Gavriel had predicted, the main thoroughfare was crowded with people, among them a considerable number of British soldiers. Some were going in and out of the different hotels, others were busy bargaining with various stall-keepers, and many soldiers were seated outside at the numerous small cafes dotting the street.

"Yona, do you remember our plan?" asked Gavriel.

"Yes, Gavriel. We will each go in separate directions. I will walk west and you will walk east, and we will meet back here in the middle in a few minutes. I need to spot a soldier or a few soldiers who look friendly and approachable."

"Excellent," said Gavriel, and the two friends headed off in opposite directions.

Sebi, who had followed the two boys all the way to the Via Egnata, watched the scene playing out in front of him with interest. He knew they were up to something, and he was determined to stay and find out. He quickly stepped inside a small coppersmith's shop where he could watch them, undetected.

In a few minutes, Gavriel and Yona met in the middle, just as they had planned. "Any luck?" Gavriel asked his friend.

"Well, yes. I saw three soldiers sitting together who look very approachable."

"Really?" said Gavriel, encouraged. His own survey of the street had yielded no positive results.

"Yes, these three soldiers are sitting together at a little table, and drinking coffee, and they are chatting and smiling. They look quite relaxed. Of course, I don't know any English so I couldn't tell what they were talking about, but it seemed pleasant, whatever they were saying."

"Great job!" said Gavriel. "Come on, show me where they are." Gavriel excitedly followed Yona.

Sebi emerged from his hiding place and followed Yona, too.

As they came near the soldiers, Yona discreetly pointed them out and whispered, "See, those three over there. Look, the broad one, with the brown curly hair, and then there's that tall one, with the high forehead, and see, the third one, with the glasses. He looks a little older, so maybe he is their superior or something."

"Yes, Yona, I see them." Gavriel observed them for a minute and concurred with Yona's impression.

"Yona, they look perfect! Wait here. Wish me luck!"

The soldiers, who had been engrossed in their conversation, looked up as Gavriel approached their table. "Hello, boy," said the older, bespectacled soldier, smiling at Gavriel.

"Hello, sir," Gavriel responded.

"Oh, do you speak English?" asked the soldier, surprised.

"Yes, sir, I do."

"How interesting," said the second soldier, the tall one with the high forehead. All three soldiers looked at Gavriel expectantly, waiting for him to say something else.

"Sirs," Gavriel began, hoping he knew enough English

to express himself clearly, "I need to buy a ticket for a ship that is leaving Salonika for England soon and I thought you might –"

The broad soldier with the curly hair interrupted and said, in an amused tone of voice, "You need to buy a ticket? For England? You are heading to England? What a coincidence. We just came from there!"

Gavriel could not tell if the soldier was just joking or if he was being made fun of. Yet he continued, undeterred.

"Yes, I am need of a ticket and I thought you might have the –"

"I might have what, an extra ticket in my trousers?" The curly-haired soldier interjected, chuckling now. Gavriel did not know how to respond and was momentarily silent.

The bespectacled soldier turned to the curly-haired one and said, "Pickwick, don't make fun of the boy. Didn't you hear him? He is asking for money. Do have a heart," he said as he stuck his hand inside the side pocket of his trousers.

"Yes, the sergeant is right, Pickwick. Give this poor street urchin some small change," agreed the tall soldier as he, too, dug some money out of his uniform.

Suddenly horrified, Gavriel realized that the soldiers had completely misunderstood what he was trying to say, and he was completely mortified as they held out their money to him. "No, no, I am not asking for your money. I don't want your money," he exclaimed in alarm.

"Oh, don't worry, boy. You can use the shilling here. I

have already bought a few things with British currency," said the sergeant as he thrust a few coins into Gavriel's hand.

"No, no, sirs, don't give me your money. That is not what I meant," Gavriel pleaded with the soldiers.

The sergeant rose from his seat, seemingly oblivious to the protestations of the boy. "Come along, Pickwick, Brown, we must be heading back to the base," he said. The other two soldiers immediately stood up and all three of them began to walk away.

Gavriel hurried over to Yona, who was waiting for him at the side of the street. "Yona, Yona, did you see what just happened? I must have said the wrong words because they didn't understand me … they gave me their money. I tried to give it back, and then they just left. I can't chase them and return it to them because they'll be insulted, maybe they'll even be angry. Oh, they just didn't understand what I was trying to say …."

"Gavriel," said Yona, who had indeed observed the entire unfortunate incident, "don't blame yourself. It was all just a terrible misunderstanding." Thinking for a minute he added, "You know, Gavriel, if it makes you feel better, we could give the money to Mr. Capon for *tzedaka*, once we get back to the orphanage."

Gavriel slowly nodded in agreement. "Actually," continued Yona, "I just realized there is something else, something important that you should do right now."

"What, Yona, what should I do?" asked Gavriel.

"I think you really must catch up to the soldiers and thank

them, for they did give you something, even though you did not ask them for it," replied his friend.

"Yes, yes, of course, you are right. I'll be back in a minute," Gavriel answered.

Gavriel quickly followed the soldiers and soon caught the eye of the older-looking one. Feeling tremendously ill at ease, he looked up at all three of them and tried to say in as pleasant voice as possible, "Thank you, sirs, for your generosity."

The sergeant looked at Gavriel. He smiled and said, "Boy, enjoy the money we gave you. Think of it as a gift from His Majesty, the King." And with that, all three soldiers quickly continued on their way.

Gavriel headed back to where Yona was waiting. Humiliated and disappointed, he said wearily, "Yona, please let's go back now, right away. I am anxious to put this whole terrible incident behind us." Yona patted his friend on the back sympathetically.

"Don't worry, I'll help you, I will. Gavriel, we will think of something else."

Gavriel did not know that at that very moment, there was someone else who was even more anxious than he was to return to the orphanage, someone in a big hurry to tell Mr. Capon all about what he had just witnessed.

Sebi.

# CHAPTER FIFTEEN

It was a clear, crisp November morning when Daniel and the rest of his battalion from the 60th 2nd/2nd London Division began the march to the Victoria Railway Station. Sergeant Pape had outlined the route they would take through the streets of London, but he did not tell them anything about their ultimate destination.

The only thing the soldiers knew was that from the station they would board a train bound for Southampton, the port in southern England, and here they would ride by boat to Le Havre, in France. Everyone assumed that they would remain in France to fight on the Western Front.

Daniel marched alongside Moishe and Avrumi; Chezki was in front of them with two other friends from the East End, Yumi Handelsman and Beinish Gordon. For the most part, all of the soldiers walked in con-templative silence, but occasionally they would chat amongst themselves or attempt a small joke.

A small number of people had gathered to acknowledge the soldiers' departure. Some waved, while others called "Good luck" and "Bless you." Daniel knew that this was a far cry from the tremendous enthusiasm that had accompanied the soldiers' departure in the fall of 1914. At the time, the war had just broken out, and the country was suffused with a tremendous patriotic spirit. As the troops had marched off to war, bands had played and throngs of people had lined the street, waving the Union Jack and cheering.

Now, two years later and countless thousands dead, the attitude to the war was considerably less enthusiastic.

As Daniel marched, he reflected on what he had just been told a little while ago. He still could not quite believe what Private Smythe had revealed to him and his friends right before they left the barracks at the Tower.

Earlier that morning, Daniel and his friends were in the large room they had shared these past two months, and they were busy packing the last-minute items their mothers had given them while they had been home on leave. They were struggling to fit all these things – tins of sardines, extra socks, crackers, sausages, chocolate, jam and candies – into their kitbags.

They did not notice Smythe as he entered the room carrying a large box. "Katz, Sheinfeld, all of you, come here a minute. I have something to give you," he said as he put down the box on an empty bed. The boys stopped what they were doing and went over to Smythe's side.

"I have been instructed to give each of you one of these," he said as he pulled out a small book from the box. "It is a special book compiled by the chief rabbi of England, Rabbi Dr. Joseph Hertz. It's a collection of contemplations for the Jewish soldier at the front. You are meant to keep it with you in your kitbags." Smythe proceeded to take them out of the box and hand them to the soldiers.

"Thank you, Smythe," said Chezki as he took the first book from Smythe's hand. The other Jewish soldiers in the room followed his example.

Once the box was empty, Smythe took it off the bed and headed out of the room. And then, abruptly, as if he had suddenly just realized that he had forgotten something, he returned to where Daniel and his friends were standing.

"I want to wish all of you the very best. I hope you will arrive safely, and will return safely."

"Thank you, Smythe," the soldiers replied without looking up, for they were all still trying to finish their last-minute packing.

"And, I would like to say, I would just like to say," said Smythe, his voice wavering slightly, "*Tzeischem l'shalom*."

"What? What was that? What did you just say?" asked Daniel, nearly dropping the jar of jam that he was holding.

"Yes, you heard me correctly. I said, '*Tzeischem l'shalom*,'" Smythe replied. By now, all eyes were fixed directly on the private. "I know this comes as a surprise to all of you, but, yes, I am Jewish." The soldiers looked at him in amazement.

Smythe continued to explain. "My name is really Feivel Smilovich. I was born here in London, but both of my parents are from Stolin, a town in Russia. When I was conscripted last January, I told them my name was 'Philip Smythe.' You see, I wasn't sure how I would manage in the army if people knew I was a Jew." Smythe paused for a minute, and then continued. "You would probably be surprised if I told you that there are a number of us Jews here like that."

The boys continued to stare at him in wonder. "I wanted to tell you that meeting you and watching the way all twelve of you have conducted yourselves here, the way you have managed to live an openly Jewish life in the army ... well, it has made a tremendous impression on me. You have given me a lot to think about." Smythe paused, and then, suddenly self-conscious, he cleared his throat and said, "In any case, I really must be going. I am sure the sergeant will be wondering what is taking me so long." And before Daniel or any of the other soldiers had a chance to say anything, Smythe was gone.

As Daniel continued marching, he couldn't stop thinking about Smythe. He found it impossible to fathom that Smythe had kept his Jewish identity a secret in the army, and he was shocked to learn that there were other soldiers like Smythe who were concealing the fact that they were Jewish.

He did not judge Smythe; Daniel's parents had taught him at an early age to be *dan l'kav zechus*, to judge people favorably, yet Smythe's revelation troubled him. But then again, Daniel thought to himself, Smythe had said he had been impressed with the way the boys from the neighborhood had conducted themselves, and that they had given him a lot to think about. Maybe, just maybe, Daniel mused, they had had a positive influence on Smythe ....

Daniel and the rest of the soldiers now began to head along Leadenhall Street. He knew that his family and the families of his friends had arranged to stand together on this street to try to catch a final glimpse of their sons and brothers. He was not sure exactly where they would be and, although he was trying to keep his gaze focused directly in front of him, his eyes began to scan the small group of people in search of his parents and his sisters.

Daniel's parents and his three sisters had been standing near the corner of Leadenhall and Lime Streets for two hours; they didn't know exactly when Daniel was scheduled to march by and they did not want to risk missing him. Yetta and Henia stood beside each other, and Devora stood between both of her parents, immediately behind her older sisters.

As usual, Mottel had spent the night baking, and under normal circumstances, he would now be at home, asleep. Today, however, was different. Although Mottel was exhausted, he was full of nervous energy, shifting his weight from one foot to the other, fixing his hat, clasping and unclasping his large hands and clearing his throat, saying, "Soon, soon, we will see Daniel soon."

Esthereva remained silent the entire time, her face immobile, almost waxen in appearance. Her eyes were fixed rigidly on the street in front of her and her right hand tightly gripped the left hand of her youngest daughter.

Devora was becoming increasingly restless and impatient. She kept complaining, "I can't see, I can't see, it isn't fair, I won't get a chance to see Daniel."

"Don't worry, Devora'le," Yetta repeatedly reassured her. "As soon as I see Daniel approaching, I will lift you up high and you can wave good-bye to him."

Henia was standing on Yetta's right side, holding a damp, crumpled handkerchief in her hand. Every few minutes, she would wipe her eyes and say quietly, more to herself than to anyone else, "Oh Daniel, where are you? Where are you?"

Yetta had spent the last two hours providing the family a running commentary of all that she saw. Continuously scanning the rows of soldiers, she would say, "Now, let's see if I can recognize anyone we know."

Finally, as a new group came into view, she said with rising excitement, "Oh, look, I think maybe I see that boy, oh, what is his name, he always comes into the bakery with his little brother, you know, the butcher's son, Handelsman, and see, over there, beside him is Beinish Gordon, you know, he was at school with Daniel and … Oh, oh, there he is, there he is! I see him, there's Daniel!"

"Where? Where is he?" Henia demanded.

"Yetta, pick me up, pick me up, I must see him," insisted Devora. Yetta scooped her little sister into her arms and lifted her up high so she could see. "Look, look, Momma, look, Papa, Yetta is right, there he is, there he is," shouted Devora excitedly as she pointed at a group of soldiers who were quickly approaching.

All eyes were riveted on Daniel as he drew closer. In just a minute or so, Daniel came into full view. Holding his rifle and bayonet firmly in his right hand, his kitbag and haversack tightly secured on his back, he stood tall and serious and was marching in step. "Daniel, Daniel, we are over here," called Devora.

For just a brief second, Daniel's eyes darted over in their direction. As if transfixed by the mere sight of him, everyone in the family became completely still. Everyone, that is, except for his mother, who brought her hand up to her cheek and slowly wiped away the single tear that had begun to slide down her face.

Just as he was about to march past, Daniel turned his head slightly to his right, as if he sensed that his father wanted to tell him something. He looked directly at his father, and their eyes met. Slowly and deliberately, the father mouthed five little words, words that he hoped would guide his son in the weeks and months ahead – "*Da lifnei Mi atah omed* (Know before Whom you stand)."

Daniel nodded almost imperceptibly and his father nodded in return, relieved that Daniel seemed to have understood the message.

And then Daniel was gone. He and the rest of the soldiers continued marching west, and soon passed Mansion House, the official residence of the Mayor of London. Here, the mayor would stand next to the entrance of the building and take the salute from the soldiers. The soldiers would then continue marching west to Fleet Street, continue south past Trafalgar Square and pass the Houses of Parliament. They would then march west on Birdcage Walk to Buckingham Palace, where they would salute the King.

Finally, they would continue south on Buckingham Palace Road to Victoria Station.

The families who had gathered to say good-bye quickly dispersed. Mothers and fathers had to return to work, and younger sisters and brothers had to return to school. The soldiers' return – if they were to return at all – would happen later, much, much later.

# CHAPTER SIXTEEN

**M**r. Capon sat behind his desk, absently playing with the rim of his fez. Sebi had just left his office, having just told him a story that he found very hard to believe.

The director of the orphanage knew full well that Sebi was far from perfect, and that he could not always be trusted to tell the truth. However, Sebi had just described a scene that he claimed to have witnessed just a short time ago with seemingly amazing accuracy.

According to Sebi, Gavriel, accompanied by Yona, had hurriedly left school that afternoon and had headed to the Via Egnata. Here, he had approached a number of British soldiers and asked for money. Sebi claimed that he had actually seen some soldiers give Gavriel money, and that Gavriel had made a point of going over to them afterwards to thank them.

After Sebi had finished telling his tale, an incredulous Mr. Capon had instructed him to find Gavriel and tell him to come to his office at once.

To Mr. Capon, all of this seemed so terribly out of character, so inexplicable. Gavriel seemed to have adjusted easily to life at the orphanage, never getting into any sort of trouble and never giving Mr. Capon any cause for concern. Then again, Mr. Capon had looked after many boys over the years, and he knew that life in an orphanage was difficult for all of them and that each of them reacted in his own way.

Suddenly, the director understood what this was all about. This strange incident must somehow be connected to Gavriel's fervent desire to go to England. Why of course! Gavriel was trying to get money for his passage on a ship. He felt so badly for the boy. Gavriel still did not know the real reason he could not go to England, and in his own mind he must have decided that it had to do with the expense of sending him. Mr. Capon realized that he must clearly explain to the boy the reason he could not travel had absolutely nothing to do with money.

In a few minutes' time, there was a weak knock on the door. "Come in," called the director. Gavriel opened the door slowly, and stood awkwardly at the entrance to the room.

"Sit down, Gavriel. I would like a word with you," said Mr. Capon.

"Yes, sir," Gavriel replied quietly, taking a seat in the small wooden chair across from the director.

"Gavriel, it has come to my attention that you and Yona went near the port this afternoon after school. Is that correct?"

"Yes, sir," Gavriel answered, his eyes downcast.

"And, Gavriel, I have been told that you were seen taking

money from a number of British soldiers." Mr. Capon paused, waiting for Gavriel to respond.

"Yes, sir, that is correct," Gavriel replied in a quiet voice.

Gavriel was not surprised that Mr. Capon had some idea of what had happened. As soon as he and Yona had returned to the orphanage an hour ago, they had been met by a widely grinning Sebi, who had informed them that he was on his way to tell Mr. Capon about all that he had seen on the Via Egnata earlier that afternoon.

"Gavriel, I must say that I find this behavior deeply distressing. Here at the Allatini Orphanage we do our very best to provide for all of our boys. No boy, under any circumstances, should ever ask anyone, anyone at all, for money. Such a practice is a disgrace, both to our fine institution and to the dignity of the boy himself." Gavriel nodded his head slightly. "Gavriel, I know that you are very anxious to go to England, and I have a feeling that your behavior today is somehow connected to this desire. Am I correct?"

"Yes, sir."

"Gavriel, I know this must be hard for you to understand, but the reason you cannot travel to England now has nothing to do with money. You must trust me," and here Mr. Capon coughed slightly, "when I tell you that there are other, more complicated reasons."

Gavriel could not possibly guess what these "other, more complicated reasons" were. All he knew was that he wanted to get to England as soon as possible, and he remained convinced that he, Gavriel, was able to play an active role in making this happen. He promised himself that later, when he was alone, he would try to think of another plan.

At the moment, though, he knew that he had to apologize to Mr. Capon. Although part of him really wanted to tell Mr. Capon the whole story – that he had gone to the Via Egnata for information about a ship and not, as Mr. Capon believed, to ask for money – he was so embarrassed about the incident and just wanted to put the whole episode behind him.

He simply said, "Mr. Capon, I am truly sorry about what happened today. It will never happen again, I promise.

"I appreciate your apology, Gavriel." The director's face then tensed slightly. "Gavriel, there is one more thing that I would like to add. I understand that Yona accompanied you this afternoon."

"Yes, he did," answered Gavriel cautiously, worried that he had gotten his friend into trouble. He did not want Yona to be blamed in any way because, after all, it had all been Gavriel's idea.

"Yona is only eleven years old, and you will soon be twelve. Yona, as you surely must know, looks up to you and respects you as, I might add, do most of the boys here. I have no doubt that by the end of today, everyone here will have heard about what transpired earlier, and therefore, although it pains me to do this, something must be done so that the other boys know that your actions did not go unpunished," said Mr. Capon. Gavriel was worried. What was Mr. Capon going to do?

"For the next two weeks, you are not allowed to leave the

immediate vicinity of the orphanage. Of course, you will continue to go to the Talmud Torah, but other than that, you must remain in this neighborhood. In two weeks time, once this unfortunate incident fades from everyone's memory, you will be allowed to walk around in the city. Is this clear?"

"Yes, Mr. Capon, I understand. But may I ask one question?"

"Yes, what is it?

"Are Yona and I still allowed to go to the *Italia Yashan* on *Shabbat*? I know he liked it so much there."

Mr. Capon was touched by Gavriel's request. He knew that attending the synagogue of their ancestors had been very important to both boys, and he did not want to deny them this experience.

"Yes, Gavriel, both of you may still attend the *Italia Yashan*. However, this is the only exception."

"Thank you, Mr. Capon."

"You may return to your room now. I trust this will be the last conversation the two of us will have about the events of this afternoon."

"Yes, sir," Gavriel said emphatically as he stood up quickly. He was even more anxious than Mr. Capon to never mention this incident again.

Mr. Capon felt greatly distressed as he watched Gavriel leave the room. He knew that at some point, probably in the not too distant future, he would have to tell Gavriel the truth, the real reason he could not go to England. And yet, Mr. Capon did not have the heart to tell this kind, thoughtful boy that his aunt and uncle in England had never responded to Mrs. Habib's letter. It was obvious to Mr. Capon that they did not want Gavriel. It was heartbreaking to see how desperately Gavriel still wanted them.

At dinner that night, Gavriel was certain that Sebi had told all the boys in the orphanage about the incident on the Via Egnata. As Gavriel began to eat his dinner of *merengena*, *pinzela* and bread sprinkled with oil, he could sense that many of them were staring at him, and he could hear a number of them whispering behind his back.

Gavriel tried his best to ignore all that was going on around him; he was trying to devise a new plan that would help him get to England. He was dismayed by the events of the afternoon but not dissuaded.

As he sat in the dining room, he reminded himself of one of his mother's favorite sayings: "*Segun el aire, se mete la vela* (Adjust the sail according to the wind)." Gavriel's mother had explained to him that this meant that when you are disappointed because something doesn't work out, you shouldn't give up. You should adapt and think of something else. In other words, Gavriel had to come up with a new idea, a new way to get information about ships bound for England. And Gavriel now knew this plan could not involve Yona, nor could it involve approaching random British soldiers on the street.

Sebi abruptly sat down beside Gavriel and, in a loud voice intended for all to hear, he demanded, "How much money did you get today?" Gavriel concentrated on eating his peas and tried to ignore Sebi. Sebi, however, did not like to be ignored, and he continued to pester Gavriel.

With a smirk on his face, Sebi continued. "Tell me, did those British soldiers give you a lot of money? Did they give you enough money to buy a ship?" Gavriel remained silent; Sebi continued to taunt Gavriel. "No, probably not. You didn't look so happy with what they gave you." His voice getting even louder and more insistent, he continued "So, come on, Mr. Leedsengland, tell me, how much did you get? Ten shillings? Twenty shillings? Ha! You're embarrassed. Did you even get enough money to buy something small, like a bag of almonds or a newspaper?" Gavriel still did not answer.

Sebi, frustrated by his inability to get a reaction from Gavriel, started to shout, "Hey, everybody, Gavriel the rich businessman is going to buy all of us a newspaper." Many of the boys squirmed uncomfortably in their seats, not sure if they should say something to try to silence Sebi. They felt terrible for Gavriel, but they were also intimidated by Sebi; they had been the victims of his bullying many times.

Yona tried in vain to silence Sebi. "Oh, come on, Sebi, let's all just forget about it."

Sebi paid no attention to Yona; he was having too much fun teasing Gavriel.

"Gavriel, Gavriel, those soldiers must have given you at least enough money for a newspaper. Come on, be nice, buy one for us. Come on, buy us a newspaper. Of course, since you are going to England, and you are so smart, you could buy us that English newspaper, and then we could all sit and listen to you translate it for us. Yes, that's a great idea, it will be such good practice for you and then …"

Suddenly, a thought occurred to Gavriel. Jumping out of his seat so quickly that he almost knocked over his dinner plate, he said, "Sebi, you have given me the most wonderful idea. I can't believe I didn't think of this earlier. How can I ever thank you? " And with that, Gavriel rushed out of the room, a broad smile on his face.

The boys in the room looked at each other, astonished by what they had just witnessed. Then all heads turned to Sebi, to see his reaction. Not knowing what else to do, Sebi took Gavriel's seat and, keeping his eyes averted from everyone, quickly helped himself to the remains of Gavriel's dinner.

The waters of the English Channel were choppy, and the ship lurched and tossed constantly. Daniel and his friends spent all of their time on the deck, despite the frigid air. They were extremely apprehensive about what awaited them in France, but they were eager to reach dry land.

After a few hours, they could dimly discern the outline of the port at Le Havre. As the ship pulled into the harbor, the battalion commander promptly ordered all of the soldiers to prepare to disembark.

As they were leaving the ship, Daniel and the rest of the boys from the East End were busy talking about Reverend Michael Adler, the British army chaplain who was stationed on the Western Front. It was known that he tried, wherever possible, to procure kosher food for the soldiers, set up *minyanim* behind the lines and arrange leave for the Jewish soldiers on *Shabbos*. The boys had even heard that in a certain small village in France, he had managed to transform an old movie house into a synagogue, and that the Jewish soldiers had nicknamed this *minyan* the "cinemagogue." All of them hoped that Reverend Adler would be able to help them in the uncertain weeks and months ahead.

After all the soldiers had disembarked, they stood at the port awaiting further instruction. The Sergeant Major, holding a megaphone, strode to the front of the battalion.

"Stand at ease! Attention! Stand at ease! Now pay attention. Corporal Stevens on me." This meant that one of the corporals, Corporal Stevens, was to come and stand beside the Sergeant Major. The corporal came to attention, shouted "Sir" and then took one pace forward. He then marched directly to the Sergeant Major and stood to his right. The Sergeant Major continued, "I will now call the names of one hundred men. These men are being sent to the Western Front to serve as reinforcements at the Somme.

"If you hear your name, fall out and reform on the marker." This meant that the men who were called were to march over to Corporal Stevens and line up behind him.

The Sergeant Major took a pair of reading glasses from his breast pocket and began to read: "Abramsky, Appleton, Bennett." The first three soldiers marched over to Corporal Stevens. "Baker, Blau, Borden, Carmichael, Collins, Colridge … Gilbert, Goldbloom, Gordon, Greene …" Daniel and his three friends quickly exchanged looks. The Sergeant Major had read four names of the twelve boys who had enlisted together. They assumed that all of their names would now be called and they would be sent as a group to the Somme. Avrumi Blau, Moishe Goldbloom and Beinish

Gordon marched over to stand behind Corporal Stevens.

The Sergeant Major continued to read, "Handelsman, Harris, Howard, Kaganoff, Katz ..." Daniel counted silently to himself, *Five ... six ... seven ...*

"Orenstein, Owens, Parker, Rand, Rickles, Ross." Daniel counted eight names. The Sergeant Major was now on the last page of the list. "Secord, Shandley, Shapiro, Skilling, Skinner, Slate, Small, Spencer, Spruce, Stafford, Teitelbaum, Thomas, Trent, Turcott ..."

Daniel counted, *Nine ... ten ...* The list ended with "Walker, Wallace, Weeks and Weitz."

The Sergeant Major removed his glasses and put them back into his pocket. It was clear that he was finished. Daniel was confused. The Sergeant Major had read out the names of eleven of the Jewish boys who had enlisted together, not twelve. Had Daniel missed hearing his name being called? *No*, he thought to himself, *the Sergeant Major had said, "Shapiro, Skilling" – his name should have immediately followed Shapiro.*

Before Daniel even had time to think about what was happening, he heard the Sergeant Major command, "Squad, stand at ease. Attention. Squad will move to the right of the column of route. Right turn. By the left. Quick march." *What was happening? His friends were leaving without him! How could this be? How could this be?*

*Why hadn't he been included with his friends? If they were headed to the Western Front, where exactly was he going?*

Daniel could hear the voice of a different sergeant now

commanding the new squad, "Left, right, left, right, left, stomach in, chest out, shoulders back, chin up ...." As Daniel watched his friends march away, he had to suppress the urge to shout, "Stop! Stop! This isn't supposed to happen." His heart was pounding and his mind was racing. *What happened to the plan? We were all supposed to stay together, help each other, look out for each other.* Daniel wanted to run after his friends, calling, "Wait for me, wait for me. Please, please don't leave me here alone."

Suddenly, the words of Reb Blau came back to haunt him. He remembered that the night before they enlisted, as they sat in the Goldblooms' front room, Reb Blau had so perceptively remarked, "The army can and will do what it wants with us." How right Reb Blau had been!

The Sergeant Major now held up a megaphone for a second time and ordered the larger, original group of men to "Pay Attention!" Daniel heard his voice, but was only vaguely aware of what he was saying. "The rest of the battalion will now march to the train station in Le Havre. You will journey to Marseilles. In Marseilles, you will board the ship *The Minnetonka*. You will arrive at the Eastern Front in approximately one week. You are being sent to Salonika. Battalion Five – advance! Left, right, left, right, swing the arms, front to rear ...."

Daniel could not believe what the Sergeant Major had just said. Salonika! He was being sent to Salonika! As he began to march to the train station, he whispered the word over and over again to himself. He hadn't even had time to adjust to the idea that he had just been separated from all of his friends, and now he was being told that he was being sent to, to … where? Salonika? Some obscure, ancient city somewhere in the Mediterranean? Salonika? Where was that? What was that? A Turkish city? A Greek city? How would he survive?

Salonika …

# PART
# TWO

*En route to Salonika*
*December 1916*

# CHAPTER EIGHTEEN

As the soldiers headed southwards by train, the mood among them was relaxed and happy. They could not believe their good luck; they were very relieved that they had managed to avoid the intense fighting of the Western Front.

The soldiers passed the time on the train eating, playing cards, reading, writing letters and singing songs, especially wartime favorites such as "Around Her Neck She Wore a Yellow Ribbon" and "It's a Long Way to Tipperary."

When the train arrived in Marseilles, the soldiers were told that they had the day to themselves and were required to meet at the port at 4 p.m. The soldiers quickly dispersed in search of the interesting sights of the city.

Daniel, who had heard that Marseilles had a sizeable Jewish community, went in search of a synagogue. He was not disappointed; without too much trouble, he was able to locate the large, historic synagogue on Rue de Breteuil, where he was able to *daven* with a *minyan*. After *Shacharis*, he managed to find out where the Jewish shops in the area were located, and he spent the rest of the day buying kosher food for the journey by ship.

As instructed, Daniel and the rest of the soldiers began to head back to the port late in the afternoon. Once all of the soldiers had been accounted for, the *Minnetonka* began its southward course on the Mediterranean Sea.

Despite their earlier high spirits, most of the soldiers found this part of the voyage very unpleasant. Many of them were extremely seasick and spent most of their time lying in the narrow cots of their hot and stuffy cabins.

Daniel spent a lot of time on deck, staring out into the horizon. He frequently found himself thinking about the story his father had told him so many months ago in the bakery – about his parents' arrival in England. He thought about how brave they had been – his mother and father – young, impoverished, with a tiny baby, crossing the sea and coming to a new country. He marveled at their courage, and he tried to draw strength from their story.

The journey was scheduled to take one week. After a number of days at sea, the *Minnetonka* sailed through the Corinth Canal. The ship then continued eastward and stopped briefly at the small Greek city of Piraeus. From here, the *Minnetonka* sailed north on the Aegean Sea and docked at the ancient city of Athens in the early morning.

The soldiers were given a day's leave in Athens. And just as he had done in Marseilles, when all the other soldiers quickly dispersed in order to go sightseeing, Daniel went in search of the Jewish neighborhood in the city.

With the help of some of the local people, Daniel soon found the Jewish area of the city called Thisson. He was directed to Meliodoni Street, where the *Etz Hayyim* synagogue was located.

Arriving at the synagogue shortly before *Shacharis*, he was warmly greeted by the men in the synagogue. Though the Romaniote service was very different from what he was used to, the familiar Hebrew words of the *tefillos* were a great comfort to him. After *Shacharis*, the *gabbai*, who introduced himself as Pini Conforti, invited Daniel to stay and have breakfast with the rest of the men. Daniel gratefully accepted the invitation, and although he did not speak Greek and could not converse with the congregants, he thoroughly enjoyed the meal.

After breakfast, the *gabbai* took hold of Daniel's arm, indicating that he wanted Daniel to come with him. He then took Daniel on a tour of the neighborhood. With evident pride, he introduced Daniel to all the men he encountered on the street, saying, "*Aftos einai o Danil. Einai Evraios stratiotis apo tin Agglia.* (This is Daniel. He is a Jewish soldier from England.)"

Pini Conforti was enormously helpful. He led Daniel to a number of stores where he was able to purchase kosher food, and he took him to the post office so that Daniel could mail a letter home to his parents. Later, he insisted on taking Daniel for lunch to his house, where Alvina, Pini's wife, greeted him warmly. Within minutes, it seemed, she managed to produce a sumptuous meal of salads, roasted vegetables wrapped in filo pastry, chickpea soup and walnut cake.

Later in the afternoon, Pini took Daniel back to the synagogue for *Mincha,* and at the end of the day Pini escorted Daniel back to the port. He wrote down his name and address on a small slip of paper and indicated that Daniel should come and visit if he should ever be in the city again. Then he embraced Daniel warmly and wished him a safe journey, a "*kalo taxidi.*"

A number of the British soldiers observed the Athenian man saying good-bye to Daniel and remarked to each other how lucky Daniel was that he had such a close relative living in the city. They would have been very surprised to learn that Daniel had met this man just a few hours ago, and that the only bond between them was that they were both Jews.

As Daniel walked up the gangplank, he reflected on the warm, hospitable Jewish community of Athens, and for the first time since he had been separated from his friends in Le Havre, his spirits lifted.

In the next few days, as the ship drew closer to its final destination, the soldiers speculated about what awaited them in Salonika. Everyone in England was under the impression that this part of the Allies' military campaign was merely a "sideshow" to the real war on the Western Front. The British public had even given the soldiers serving here the epithet, "The Gardeners of Salonika." Public opinion was that there was little or no active warfare in the area, and all the British soldiers did there was dig trenches and put up defensive barbed wire around the city.

However, the city itself was considered volatile and

unstable. Soldiers had heard reports of unchecked cases of malaria and typhoid and had been told that the city experienced madly fluctuating extremes in temperature – unbearable heat in the summer months and fierce extremes of cold in the winter. The impression among them, in general, was that Salonika was a dangerous, dirty city, a city in constant flux, and that it was a mixture of constantly warring Turks and Greeks.

The only thing Daniel knew about the city was what he recalled hearing many years ago, though he couldn't remember when. He thought that perhaps Rabbi Shlomo Alkabetz, the poet who had composed *Lecha Dodi*, had been born in Salonika. Daniel reasoned to himself that if this were true, it was proof that at least at some point there had been a Jewish presence in the city. Daniel hoped that once his regiment arrived in Salonika he would have some time to explore the city and find out.

From Athens to Salonika the ship proceeded slowly and cautiously along the rocky little islands of the Aegean Sea, and finally, early one December morning, the harbor came into view.

As the ship slowly neared the port, it was met by British military destroyers and escorted into the bay in response to the constant threat of being torpedoed by German submarines in the Mediterranean.

Daniel and a number of other soldiers were standing on the deck wearing their army-issue greatcoats and woolen caps, for it was now quite cold. In the soft purple and pink hues of the early morning, they could discern a wide, horseshoe-shaped bay, surrounded by steep hills and tall trees. As the sun continued to rise, the soldiers could see small colorful houses nestled among the hills, numerous white domes adorning the Greek churches and tall white minarets rising high above the city slopes.

Soon, an imposing white stone edifice, known to many in the city as *"La Tour Blanca* (The White Tower)" came into view. It loomed large at the eastern end of the wide promenade that curved around the bay.

The ship dropped anchor about half a mile from the shore, and the soldiers were taken by small tugs to the port. The port was crowded with small supply ships, French and British battleships, fishing boats, army hospital ships and commercial boats of all sizes and shapes, their prows sticking over onto the wide street.

Daniel surveyed the crowded port. He saw soldiers in a variety of uniforms, fishermen hauling their catches in wide barrels, army nurses hurriedly returning to their hospital ships, stevedores carrying huge wooden crates and a number of young boys selling newspapers.

One newspaper boy stood at the port and observed the arrival of the British soldiers with particular interest. He had been standing in one spot for quite a while, watching the soldiers get out of the tugs as they reached the shore.

For the past two weeks, the boy had been selling the English paper *The Daily Star* at the port. He decided, in fact, to begin selling newspapers for this very reason – so that he would have a reason to interact with the British soldiers and hopefully, through his contact with them, manage to find out about ships bound for England.

One by one he surveyed the soldiers, hoping to find what, exactly, he was not yet sure. He hoped that maybe one of these newly arrived soldiers held the key; maybe one of them, somehow, in some way, would be able to help him. Perhaps, Gavriel thought to himself, I am finally on the right track.

# CHAPTER NINETEEN

**M**uch to Daniel's dismay, the soldiers were not allowed to spend any time in Salonika. As soon as all of them had disembarked, they were immediately ordered to begin marching to Summerhill Camp, the main British camp in the area.

As the soldiers headed west, they saw a number of French and British steamers lying vacant; these ships had been run ashore after being torpedoed by German submarines a few months earlier. The soldiers heard enemy aircraft overhead a number of times, and they were ordered to scatter and lay flat on the ground until it was deemed safe for them to continue marching.

This was the soldiers' first indication that the war here was not as uneventful as many people in Britain seemed to think; and, as the next twenty-four hours would demonstrate, conditions here were considerably harsher than most of the soldiers had been led to believe.

Summerhill Camp was situated atop a barren open plain that gradually sloped from the surrounding hills to the sea. From a distance, it was surrounded by numerous snow-capped mountains. The largest among them, some fifty miles southwest of the camp, was Mount Olympus, rising over 9,500 feet high.

The soldiers completed the grueling seven-mile march in the early evening and reached the camp around dinnertime. After a simple meal, they were assigned to their tents and were provided with blankets and groundsheets. They were told to be ready for breakfast at 8 a.m. the next morning, to be followed by full military inspection at 9 a.m. Almost all of the soldiers went to sleep early that night, exhausted by the day's exertions.

That night, a terrible winter storm descended on Summerhill Camp. A furious and penetrating wind – infamously known as "the Vardar Blast" – blew off of the Vardar River in the northwest and swept across the flat plain of the camp.

In the middle of the night, the soldiers were awakened by the howl of the wind and the wild shaking of their tents. They ran outside in the sleet and the hail and frantically tried to secure the ropes of their tents, but they were no match for the ferocious strength of the storm. Many of the tents came loose from the ropes and blew away, the canvas ripped to shreds by the sheer force of the wind.

As the wind whipped blankets, sheets and clothing around their heads, the soldiers, now completely soaked through, chased after the tents. Furniture overturned and chairs and tables flew through the air and fell to the ground, sticking in the quagmire of mud that soon surrounded the camp. Although the soldiers tried to help each other, shouting,

"Over here, over here," the incessant roar of the wind made it impossible for them to hear each other's voices.

In the early hours of the morning, the storm finally abated. The soldiers, Daniel among them, crammed themselves into the few tents that had remained standing and somehow managed to fall asleep.

When Daniel awoke a few hours later, he found himself lying on the bare ground of a tent, surrounded by thirty or so other men. It was very early; Daniel had trained himself to wake up at 6:30 every morning to allow himself time to *daven*.

Daniel felt as if his entire body was frozen, and as his hand brushed the ground, he realized that the earth was covered with a light dusting of snow. When he exhaled, he could see his breath forming small white circles in the cold air. He tried to shake the numbness out of his arms and legs, but it took him a few minutes before he was able to stand up properly.

Shivering, his teeth chattering so loudly he was amazed that he didn't waken anyone, Daniel quickly got dressed. He then took the water bottle that was attached to his kitbag and poured some ice cold water on his bare hands, almost gasping from the pain as the frigid water splashed onto his fingers.

Daniel opened up his kitbag, thankful that he had been able to hold onto it last night. He was surprised to see that his *tefillin* bag was not in its usual spot at the top. *Could it have fallen to the bottom of the bag?* he wondered. Daniel slowly emptied his kitbag, but the *tefillin* weren't there. He was confused. He didn't remember his bag blowing open last night. But maybe it had and he just hadn't noticed. Maybe the *tefillin* had indeed fallen out and then someone else had closed the bag later on? If this was the case, where were his *tefillin*?

He hurried out of the tent and began to search the area around him. The ground was littered with debris and personal belongings that had been tossed around by the storm. Daniel didn't know where to look first. Frantically, he walked around the area, turning over blankets, sheets, clothing and broken pieces of furniture, hoping to find his *tefillin*. Soon he began to hear the sounds of the other soldiers stirring. He knew that it was almost time for breakfast and that he would soon be expected in the mess tent.

Frustrated, Daniel sat down on a torn piece of canvas. He tried to remember his actions of the previous night, but all he could recall was a frightening blur of rain, wind and utter confusion.

It suddenly occurred to him that maybe, in fact, he had left his *tefillin* in Athens, at the synagogue. Perhaps, distracted by meeting the friendly *gabbai*, he had neglected to take his *tefillin* bag with him as he left the synagogue. He tried to remember – did he have it with him when he walked through the streets of Athens? Was he carrying it in his hands? Or had he in fact placed it back in his kitbag? Daniel just didn't know.

By now, all of the other soldiers were awake and dressed and had started to walk to the mess tent. Soon it would be time for inspection. Daniel knew that he had no choice but to start to *daven*, even without his *tefillin*. He stood up slowly.

Facing east, with the sound of the cruel Vardar wind still roaring in his ears, Daniel sadly said *Shacharis*.

Throughout the day, Daniel was distracted by thoughts of his lost *tefillin*. Perhaps he could write Pini Conforti a letter and ask him to look for them at the synagogue in Athens. But then again, the *gabbai* didn't understand English, and even if someone could translate a letter for him, why put the man to the trouble if the *tefillin* had really been lost here, at Summerhill Camp?

Should he write his parents and tell them that he had lost his *tefillin*? Maybe they could send him another pair? No, *tefillin* was far too expensive to be sent in the mail. And furthermore, Daniel knew that if his parents were to learn that their son had lost his *tefillin*, they would be very upset. Daniel remembered his father's joy the day he had bought Daniel his *tefillin*, a few months before Daniel's *bar mitzvah*. No, no, his parents must not know that his *tefillin* had been lost.

Maybe the *tefillin* were still here, somewhere at the camp. But where? The wind could have blown the *tefillin* hundreds of miles away, or they could be lying in the mud somewhere. Would the *tefillin* still be kosher, even if Daniel managed to find them?

If only one of his friends were with him, Daniel thought miserably to himself. At least then he could borrow his, until he had this sorted out. His only option, he finally realized, was to somehow get to the city of Salonika and see if he could purchase *tefillin* there.

Daniel was so engrossed in his thoughts that he did not hear his name being called after lunch. The second time his name was called and he did not respond, a number of the other soldiers nudged him and said, "Sheinfeld, the brass wants you!" Daniel was worried. Why would one of his superiors want to speak to him? Maybe someone had seen him earlier that morning scrounging around the camp and had reported his unusual behavior? Or perhaps the sergeant had noticed that Sheinfeld was not concentrating on drill that morning and he was about to be disciplined?

Daniel quickly approached the sergeant. The sergeant virtually barked at Daniel. "Sheinfeld, report to Officer Jones at once. Dismissed." Daniel hurried over to the officers' tent. The flaps to the tent were open and the officer noticed Daniel right away.

"Come in, Private," instructed the officer. Daniel stepped into the tent and initiated the salute. He then stood awkwardly at attention. "At ease," instructed the officer.

The officer sat behind a large desk and held a piece of paper in his hand. Appearing to read from the sheet, he said, "Now, Private Sheinfeld is it, Daniel Sheinfeld?"

"Yes, sir," answered Daniel, feeling nervous.

"Sheinfeld, I have here a note from a certain Sergeant Pape, from London. Says he trained you, at the Tower, a number of months ago. He says he thinks you have the makings of an excellent soldier. He says you are fit, fast and intelligent. Yes, it looks like you made quite an impression on Pape."

Daniel was surprised to hear this. Pape had seemed to dislike all of the Jewish boys from the East End. But then, Daniel suddenly remembered the seemingly odd conversation he had had with him right before they were shipped out, when Pape had asked him a number of questions about what he had done before Daniel had enlisted.

The officer continued. "Private Sheinfeld, I am sending you to a course. You are going to learn how to be a signaler. You will learn Morse code and how to use a heliograph. The training is done here, at Camp Summerhill. It is an intensive course and it will take a month."

Daniel's face registered evident displeasure, realizing that if he had to remain at the camp for an entire month, he would not be able to go to Salonika to buy *tefillin*. Noticing the look on the young soldier's face, the officer said, in an almost fatherly tone, "Don't be concerned, Sheinfeld. Pape would not have recommended you if he did not think you were qualified. The course begins tomorrow morning. Report here after breakfast. That is all. Dismissed."

Daniel hesitated slightly, for army protocol dictated that he was not to speak to a superior after he had been dismissed. But he knew that he must ask his question.

Cautiously, he said, "Attention, sir. Permission to ask a question, sir?"

"Yes, Sheinfeld? You have something to add?"

Daniel continued uneasily. "Sir, is it possible that before the course begins, I might have a few hours in the city, in Salonika?" The officer looked quizzically at the private. This was a most unusual request. After all, Sheinfeld had arrived at the camp just the night before. Why did he immediately need a leave?

"Sheinfeld, what business do you have in the city?" asked the officer.

"Sir, I have lost an important religious item and I had hoped to replace it, that is, to purchase another one, in Salonika."

"Impossible, Sheinfeld," the officer replied, "simply impossible. The course begins tomorrow morning. You will have to wait until you finish the course to go to the city. In one month's time, I will grant you a day's pass to Salonika. Surely you can wait one month to purchase whatever it is that you need. A month is not a long time. Dismissed."

Realizing that he could not say anything else or he would risk being considered insubordinate, Daniel quickly saluted the officer and left the tent.

As he slowly walked away, Daniel felt even more despondent than he had earlier in the day. He had to wait a month before he could go to Salonika. An entire month! The officer was completely wrong; to Daniel, a month without his *tefillin* seemed like an eternity.

Salonika
December 1916

# CHAPTER TWENTY

G avriel had it all planned. He and the rest
of the class were getting out of school
early today because their *rubi* had an important
meeting somewhere in the city that afternoon.
While all of the other boys were making plans
to spend the afternoon playing *cuexcos*, Gavriel
had something else in mind entirely.

After watching the British soldiers arrive
last week and head for Summerhill Camp,
Gavriel had decided to go the camp himself.
He had heard that it was very large and that
hundreds of British soldiers were stationed
there. He was certain that a number of them
would be interested in buying the latest edi-
tion of *The Daily Star*, and that in the process, he could engage at least one of them in
a conversation about ships scheduled to sail
to England.

He did not tell Yona where he was going.
Even though he did not foresee any problems
with this new idea, he did not want to impli-
cate his best friend just in case something
unexpected happened. He simply told Yona
that he had something important to do after

school. Although Yona was curious, he respected Gavriel's privacy and did not ask him where he was going.

Gavriel, carrying his kaleidoscope and armed with a bag of newspapers, hurried to the port after school and started walking west. It was a long walk, and to pass the time, he frequently took out his kaleidoscope and held it up to the winter sun. He loved looking at all of the shifting images and colors; he never tired of seeing all of the subtle changes that he produced just by the tilt of his hand as he held the kaleidoscope up to the light.

As Gavriel walked, he thought about what he was going to say once he reached Summerhill Camp. After the disastrous experience down at the Via Egnata, Gavriel knew he had to make sure that this time the English soldiers clearly understood what he was saying. "Sir, would you know of a ship sailing to England in the next few days or weeks?" and "Thank you kindly for the information," Gavriel said to himself, over and over.

After walking up and down the small hills for over an hour, Gavriel began to tire. The bag of newspapers was beginning to feel heavy, and Gavriel's feet had started to hurt. He tried his best to distract himself by looking around at his surroundings – the small wooded hills, the stone huts of the ancient Greek villages, the wide ravines and the occasional meandering goat.

As Gavriel began to ascend the largest hill, he saw a number of British army trucks ahead of him. Encouraged, he picked up his pace.

After climbing the hill for almost two hours, Gavriel reached the top. Immediately, he saw a wide wooden sign that read "Welcome to Camp Summerhill" affixed to a large gate. Gavriel stood and stared at the sign, pleased with himself that he had finally managed to reach the camp.

Suddenly, a loud voice boomed down at him. "WHO GOES THERE?" Startled by the voice, Gavriel jumped. He looked around, but he didn't see anyone. He didn't answer. The voice boomed again: "WHO GOES THERE?" Gavriel looked around a second time, but still did not know where the voice was coming from. Then, for a third time, the voice demanded, "Identify yourself immediately or I will shoot." Gavriel was very frightened.

Not knowing where to look, he raised his face to the sky and shouted, "I am Gavriel Florentin."

"Do not move. Stay where you are," commanded the disembodied voice. Gavriel did as he was instructed and remained rooted to the spot. In a matter of seconds, a tall burly soldier, his annoyance marked clearly on his face, marched over toward Gavriel.

"Boy," he shouted, even though by now he was standing just a few feet away from him, "this is a British Army Camp, and I am the sentry on duty. I demand to know what are you doing here!"

Gavriel, trying not to seem scared, said quietly, "I came to sell newspapers to the soldiers." And with that, he quickly retrieved one from his bag to show the sentry.

"Selling newspapers? Here? At the camp? Boy, are you soft

in the head?" snapped the sentry. Gavriel remained silent. "This is no place for a child. This is an army camp! Don't you understand what that means?" As if to emphasize the point, the soldier moved his rifle ever so slightly in Gavriel's direction.

The sentry continued. "Boy, you are supposed to be in school, not wandering about the countryside trying to sell newspapers. Now listen to me, and listen closely. You are to leave this instant. If I ever, ever see you again at this camp, or anywhere near this camp, for that matter, I will drag you by the ears to my commanding officer. And believe me, I assure you, you do not want that to happen. Now go away. Go home. Get out." The sentry glared at Gavriel.

Gavriel did not understand everything the sentry had just said, but he had understood enough. He immediately started to run, and kept on running until he was certain that he was out of the sentry's line of vision. Panting loudly, he scrambled down the large hill.

Tired now, Gavriel began to drag his feet. He felt very disappointed and discouraged. Again, his plans had failed.

Soon, Gavriel noticed that it was starting to get dark, and he knew that he could not risk being late getting back to the orphanage. Despite his exhaustion, Gavriel forced himself to pick up his pace. As he did so, his mother's words rang in his ears again: "*Segun el aire, se mete la vela.* (Adjust the sail according to the wind.)" And, although he did not feel like it at the moment, he hoped that tomorrow, after he had had a good night's sleep, he would think of yet another plan.

The tall dark-haired man, dressed in a heavy woolen overcoat and a black felt hat, walked slowly along New Road, looking carefully at all of the buildings. He was not from London, and he was not familiar with the neighborhood. When he had arrived at the train station, he had made a few inquiries and had been told that the best place for him to go would be Sheinfeld's Bakery. Sure enough, as the man continued walking north, a large shop with elegantly styled black letters painted on the window soon came into view.

As the man pushed open the front door, the welcoming aroma of freshly baked bread immediately filled his nostrils. He saw that the shop was very busy. As the war had dragged into its third year, the government introduced strict rationing of staples, such as flour and sugar, and there was frequently a shortage of basic food items. As a result, the stores were always crowded with people hoping to buy whatever was available that day.

There was a long line at the counter. Two young women were busy serving the customers.

CHAPTER TWENTY-ONE

The man looked at the women and could tell immediately from their similar coloring – light blonde hair and fair complexions – that they were sisters. He waited patiently, and after a few minutes, he reached the front of the line.

"May I help you, sir?" asked one of the sisters, who looked to be about fifteen years old.

"Yes, I hope so," the man replied. "I have heard that this shop has a message board, some sort of wall where people are able to post messages and announcements, things like that. Is this correct?"

"Yes, sir, it is over there," she said, motioning to the back of the store. "My mother is standing right beside it, over there. Can you see her?"

"Yes, yes, thank you very much, young lady."

The young woman noticed that the stranger had an unusual accent, one she could not remember ever hearing before. This was odd; the people who came in and out of the bakery to make use of the message board were always people they knew from the neighborhood. She wondered if the man was in the right place.

In the past few months, the Sheinfeld's bakery had gradually become a center of communication for Jewish soldiers and their families. It had all started when one of their neighbors, the Weitz family, had decided to move to Manchester.

Their son Pesach, one of the eleven neighborhood boys who had been sent to the Somme, was due home soon on leave and his parents had been unable to contact him and give him their address. They asked Mottel if they could hang up a message for Pesach at the bakery. Of course, Mottel did not mind. He knew how hard it was to have a son in the army, and he gladly hung up the note on the back wall of the shop. When Pesach came home and Mottel saw him in the neighborhood, he told him that he had a note waiting for him at the bakery.

Soon, other people in the neighborhood starting coming to the bakery and asking Mottel if they could also leave notes and notices for the soldiers. Communication was difficult; most people still did not have telephones, and letters sent overseas could sometimes take a long time to reach the soldiers at the front.

Word quickly spread among the soldiers that the bakery was the place to go if you wanted to leave or pick up a message, and soon enough, many Jewish soldiers on leave in London for a few days would come and check the back wall of the shop.

The tall dark-haired man headed toward the older woman at the back. "Excuse me, ma'am," he said. "Would you be so kind as to allow me to hang up a photograph of a young boy on your wall?" The woman looked at the man with surprise. He did not look at all familiar to her, and his accent was most unusual.

"Sir, are you sure you are in the right place?" she asked.

"I believe so, ma'am. I was told that you and your family allow people in the neighborhood to hang up messages at the back of your store and that many Jewish soldiers frequent your bakery. I have here, here, in my pocket," and with this he withdrew a small picture, "the photograph of a young boy. I was hoping that perhaps one of the Jewish soldiers, while here on leave, might recognize him. You see, he is missing and we don't know how to … We have not heard from him and –" Here the man's voice started to break. He stopped talking and cleared his throat, trying to compose himself.

"Oh, my," said the woman, her tone now sympathetic. "Of course, you may. Here, let me clear a space. We will put it right here, in the middle." The woman quickly affixed the photograph to the wall, as well as the accompanying message carefully written in bold block letters: "HAVE YOU SEEN THIS BOY?"

"Sir, please leave me your name and telephone number, that is, if you have a telephone. If anyone recognizes the boy in the photo, I will contact you immediately," said the woman.

"Thank you, thank you. I cannot tell you how much I appreciate your help," replied the man. He took out a small piece of paper and a pencil, and quickly wrote down his name, address and telephone number. The woman tucked the paper into the front pocket of her dress.

The man turned to leave, but then, as if he had just reminded himself of something, turned back to the woman and said, "One more thing, please, if it is not too much to ask of you." In an almost plaintive tone he said, "If possible, could you ask the customers to be careful with the photo. You see –" and here the man's voice began to break again, "it is the only one we have …."

"Yes, yes, of course, I will do my utmost to make sure that it is safe," the woman reassured the stranger.

The man tipped his hat in her direction and promptly left the bakery, hoping not to miss the train going home.

*Summerhill Camp*
*March 1917*

# CHAPTER TWENTY-TWO

**D**aniel had completed his month-long course and was now officially a signaler in the British Army. He had learned Morse code and how to operate a heliograph.

When Daniel first saw the heliograph, it reminded him of a very large kaleidoscope, a toy he remembered his sisters playing with years ago. Both devices were similar; though one was meant for a child and the other was designed for military communication, they both relied on mirrors and sunlight, and both could be used to create different patterns by combining these elements. The kaleidoscope and the heliograph were instruments of perception, altered by the manipulation and the perspective of the individual.

Daniel had spent the month of training waiting to go to Salonika to replace his lost *tefillin*, and now that the month was over, he assumed that the warrant officer would grant him a day's pass. However, it appeared that the officer had forgotten about it completely, and as the days turned into weeks, Daniel still had not been given leave.

He knew that army regulation prohibited him from approaching the warrant officer directly, and he was not friendly enough with anyone at the camp to request them to ask the officer for him. Daniel thought about Smythe, or "Smilovich," and fondly remembered the soldier's amazing ability to always know what was about to happen next and his willingness to share this information with Daniel and his friends.

The rumor at the camp was that once the weather improved, an attack on the Central Powers situated around Lake Doiran was planned. There had been a stalemate in the region since November, as the exceedingly harsh weather conditions had made all military operations impossible. However, everyone seemed to know that very soon they would advance to the west in an attempt to surprise the Bulgarian army and capture a number of hills. Daniel knew that at this time, his newly acquired skills as a signaler would be called upon.

As the weeks passed, Daniel began to feel increasingly weary. The howl of the Vardar Blast disturbed his sleep, and Daniel frequently woke up in the middle of the night, shivering. He developed a persistent cough and began to feel cold all of the time, even during the day.

Adding to Daniel's discomfort was the fact that since his arrival at Summerhill, he had been unable to eat most of the food. He subsisted on tea sweetened with a bit of sugar, tack biscuits, tins of condensed milk, watery oatmeal and the occasional fruits and vegetables. As a result, Daniel had lost a lot of weight, and his once well-fitting uniform now hung loosely on his undernourished frame.

Daniel increasingly missed his friends and his family. Although the soldiers at the camp were cordial to him and were generally respectful of his religious practices, Daniel kept to himself and did not socialize with the other soldiers, most of whom spent their leisure time playing football and singing in the amateur choir.

Daniel spent almost of his time alone. He was very lonely, and fervently wished that at least one of his friends had been sent to Salonika with him. To pass the time, he wrote a lot of letters, always reassuring his parents that he was managing and that he was feeling fine – desperately hoping that they could not detect the truth between these lines.

The one bright spot for Daniel was receiving mail – the letters and occasional parcels his family sent him from London. He knew that strict rationing was now in effect, and he was tremendously appreciative of anything that they sent him – a few chocolate bars, a tin of biscuits, some jam. Daniel particularly enjoyed reading Devora's letters; she wrote him all about the news in the neighborhood, and she never failed to finish her letters with the same question: "Have you found our mission yet?"

Daniel always humored her when he wrote back, telling her that no, unfortunately, he had not as yet found their mission, but that she was not to worry because he was certain it would be soon be revealed to both of them.

One morning shortly after weapons drill, Daniel returned to his tent and saw that he had two pieces of mail on his bed.

One letter was certainly from Devora; he recognized her childish, uneven handwriting immediately. The other letter seemed to be larger; it was stuffed into an envelope bearing what appeared to be a French postmark.

Daniel opened the letter from Devora first. As usual, it was full of news about his parents and his sisters, her teachers and her friends. And of course, it ended with Devora's query about their mission. With a smile, Daniel put the letter back on his bed and picked up the other piece of mail.

Daniel noticed that the writing on this envelope was irregular, as if it had been written with a shaky hand. Yet somehow, the writing was familiar to Daniel. Could it be a letter from Reb Blau, from Avrumi? Still standing, Daniel excitedly tore open the envelope.

Had he known what Avrumi had written, Daniel would have certainly sat down before he started to read.

# From the Western Front

# CHAPTER TWENTY-THREE

BS"D
*February 11, 1917*

*Dear Daniel,*
*I am writing you this letter aboard the hospital ship, the* Warilda. *I am being invalided home and am bound for England.*

*I haven't seen you in many months, and I do not know what it has been like for you on your own in Salonika. The few reports that reach us here say that there is very little fighting there, and that the worst you encounter is extreme cold and boredom. Daniel, you do not know how* Hashem *blessed you by sending you to the east and sparing you the horrors of the Western Front.*

*It is hard – almost too hard – to tell you about all that has happened to your friends, but I feel that you would want to know what has happened to us.*

*After we were separated from you at Le Havre, we were driven north and then west, by cattle trucks. The French countryside was beautiful – clear blue skies, gently rolling wooded hills, trees resplendent in orange and red leaves, all reflected in the soft autumn light.*

*We were taken to a small army camp, and as soon as we saw the soldiers who had returned from the front lines, the beauty of the French countryside completely vanished from our minds.*

*These soldiers were the lucky ones, if such a thing could be said about them. They had managed to stay alive, but only a few, a very few, appeared to be unscathed. Most of the men were broken beyond repair — bandaged, bloodied, crippled; many were lying motionless on narrow cots — silent, numb, eternally shaken.*

*We thought we understood by looking at these men what awaited us, but we were wrong. Not one of us could have possibly imagined the horrors of the front line.*

*After a number of days we were taken to the Ancre River, a small tributary that flows through the northern sector of the battlefield. As we came closer to the front line, we began to feel the ground tremble, and soon, it was impossible to tell the difference between sound and vibration. Our bodies shook from fear. In the distance we could hear the noise of exploding bombs, guns roaring like drums, and continuous echoes.*

*We descended into what would be our home for the next few days — the trenches.*

*The trenches. Long dark nights spent in mud and filth. Endless days standing in rainwater up to our knees. Besieged by rats, frogs, lice, beetles, as Yosef was besieged by scorpions and snakes in the pit. These trenches, these angry scars slashed into the ground, swallowed us up and almost consumed us. They were deeper than the height of a full-grown man and surrounded by a protective wall of earth, called the parapet.*

*We were cold, we were filthy, and we waited and waited.*

There was little to do – we cleaned our rifles, checked our packs and wrote letters.

Sometimes the Germans would send over trench mortars – explosives aimed directly into the trenches. If we were lucky, a sentry would spot the black speck of the mortar bomb and he would blow his whistle in warning. Everyone would crouch down low, even deeper into the muck and filth, hoping to avoid the devastating explosion. Later, when it was over, we would be busy tending to those injured in the attack and repairing the trenches.

We were hungry all the time. Although the food was supposed to be brought up to the front by truck or horse and cart, many times it didn't arrive. When it did, there was little of it that we could eat. There was some kosher food at the base, but it never reached us. We relied on bits of dried fruit, tins of "tack biscuits," jam and tea that had a distinctly foul taste.

The night before we were set to go over the top, all of us were scared, quiet and nervous. Most of us didn't sleep, for we knew by now that our chances of surviving active war were slim. I stared up at the stars and thought of my parents and my younger brothers at home in London, and of you, somewhere in Salonika. I was comforted by the fact that all of you were far away from this nightmare.

We davened, we davened so very much.

The next morning at 7:30 a.m., the Officer gave a sharp blow on his whistle, signaling the start of the attack. We were commanded to "go over the top" – to climb out over the parapet on ladders.

Chezki climbed out first. I followed, and assumed Moishe was behind me. What I did not know until later, much later, was that Moishe did not follow. Moishe did not climb out, not then and not ever. He remained in the trench, paralyzed by fear.

As soon as we climbed out, we were met by a hurricane of small arms fire. Many men were killed or wounded instantly. The officer yelled, "Come on, men, be British," and we immediately formed the line, as we had been trained to do.

We began to walk forward. We were loaded down with all of our equipment, and as we slowly advanced toward no man's land, we were easy targets for the German machine gunners. We had been ordered to never, ever stop, to never move out of the way of the enemy artillery — we had been instructed to walk steadily toward the enemy. As we walked into the fire, we could hear the noise of shellfire, machine gun bullets, explosions and screaming, endless, endless screaming.

Within seconds, entire lines of men fell, their wounded bodies collapsing on the ground like rag dolls. The dead and the wounded lay together, spattered with shrapnel, riddled with bullets, the earth a sickening mixture of khaki and red. Many men would lie where they had fallen for a number of hours, writhing and shrieking in pain.

The entire assault was over in a matter of minutes. The destruction it wreaked will last a lifetime.

There was smoke everywhere. It was impossible to see, and I quickly lost sight of Chezki. Later, I learned that during our attempted advance, he was hit by a flying piece of shrapnel and fell into a shell hole. He remained in no man's land for hours, his right shoulder bleeding copiously. Eventually, he was able to crawl back closer to the line. After many hours Chezki, now suffering from acute shock, was spotted by a stretcher-bearer and was carried to the field dressing station.

Daniel, before Chezki could be transferred behind the lines to the hospital, he succumbed to his wounds.

There is a military cemetery nearby – the Ancre British Cemetery. It lies two kilometers south of the village of Beaumont Hamel, just west of the railway and the river. Off to the side is a small Jewish cemetery. I have committed its location to memory so that I may be able to tell Chezki's parents exactly where their son lies.

Two days after the assault, a number of us were given permission to leave the front, and we gathered at the cemetery. The rabbi on the Western Front, Reverend Michael Adler, said Kaddish for Chezki and the others. It was clear from the look on Reverend Adler's face and from the sound in his voice that he had said Kaddish far too many times.

Reverend Adler took a picture of the kever to send home to Chezki's parents. A small white Magen David marks the spot.

I gathered Chezki's personal effects to be sent home – his siddur and tefillin, the letters and photos his family had sent him, and a small notebook.

In the trenches, Chezki had spent a lot of time writing in this notebook, and I looked inside it now. Believe it or not, it was full of all kinds of ideas, business plans, for when he would return to England. But then again, this probably does not surprise you. Chezki always had big plans, so many plans ....

Moishe is suffering from something they call "shell shock" – a *nervous condition for which there is no certain cure. He has a strange, vacant look on his face and remains unresponsive to everything around him. No one knows if he will recover or if,* chas v'shalom, *he will remain like this permanently. He has been sent home and is now in a military hospital somewhere on the outskirts of London.*

*Of our original group of twelve, three of us remained after the first assault – me, Orenstein and Weitz. Of the other eight who enlisted with us there is also much to be written, but not now. Some were never found, and they are listed as "missing, presumed killed."*

*Those of us who survived the assault were sent further north along the Ancre River, near the village of Grandcourt. There was a rotation of sorts – four to seven days in the trenches, short breaks back at the camp and then a return to the trenches.* Baruch Hashem, *Orenstein, Weitz and I managed to stay together.*

*A number of weeks ago, as a result of my standing in the trenches in socks that were perpetually soaked through, I developed what they call "trench foot." In the past ten days, my feet have become horribly infected. I was sent to the field hospital, where I was told that both of them are now septic and that the infection is so great that I may lose one or both feet. The doctor there decided to send me home to England for treatment.*

*Now, only Orenstein and Weitz remain from our original group.*

*Daniel, I must tell you that the Avrumi you knew – the one you grew up with, the one you played with, the one who sat beside you at* cheder – *he is gone. Gone.*

*For years, you and all the others in the neighborhood thought that I was the one who had all the answers. But not now, not anymore. Daniel – I have no more answers – I don't understand anything. All that I have now are questions – endless, endless questions.*

*Please, Daniel, please be careful. Stay well, stay safe, and know that you are always in my thoughts.*

*Your friend, Avrumi*

As the words of what he had just read started to sink in, Daniel began to feel dizzy and nauseous. Chezki is gone? Buried in France? Other boys are missing? Moishe ... shell-shocked? And Avrumi, he may never walk again .... *Ribbono shel Olam* ... How can this be? How can this be ...?

Daniel collapsed to the ground.

Private Munroe returned to this tent, humming happily to himself. He was in a good mood – it was a beautiful spring day and he had just received a large package from home. As he opened the flaps to the tent that he shared with nine other soldiers, he was horrified by what he saw. Dropping his package – its contents breaking and scattering noisily on the ground – he ran back out of the tent and began to shout frantically, "Medic! Medic! I need a medic!"

# PART
# THREE

# CHAPTER TWENTY-FOUR

As the weeks passed, Gavriel appeared to be his usual self – happy, optimistic and confident. Only Yona, Gavriel's closest friend, knew that Gavriel was becoming increasingly impatient. After all, as Gavriel frequently told him, he had been in the orphanage now for six entire months, despite the fact that Mrs. Habib had originally told him that he would only be there "for a little while."

Although Gavriel could hear his mother's voice clearly telling him, "*La ventura, por quien la percura* (Good fortune happens to those who try)," he simply could not think of anything else that he could do. He did not want to ask Mr. Capon again about when he would be going to England because he was still embarrassed about the incident on the Via Egnata, and he did not want to remind the director about it.

Gavriel continued to sell newspapers in the neighborhood, but he soon realized that most people who bought a paper were usually in a hurry and had little or no interest in talking to a newspaper boy. And he knew from experience that he could neither simply approach a soldier on the street for information nor attempt to talk to one of soldiers stationed at Camp Summerhill.

One afternoon, a number of the older boys organized a ring-toss game in the small courtyard behind the orphanage. The boys placed a large wooden board that had nails protruding from its surface atop a few discarded crates. Then the boys distributed a few iron rings, and everyone had a turn throwing the rings, trying to land them over the nails. The boys who managed this would win a few coveted *cuexcos*.

Yona and Gavriel joined in the game; Yona loved to play and his aim was excellent. In a matter of minutes, Yona had won a number of *cuexcos*. Now it was another boy's turn to try his luck. The boy, Sabatino, was new to the orphanage, and he had never played before. He quickly grabbed the iron ring, and in his enthusiasm he reached his hand behind him so suddenly that he almost hit another boy, Rachamim, in the face.

"*Ay, cuidate* (Hey, watch it)!" chided Rachamim. "If you keep winding up like that, you're going to knock out my eye! I could end up in the hospital!"

"Yeah," said Mercado, another boy who had been standing nearby. "I can just imagine the scene! All of us marching into that nice big building to visit Rachamim. I am sure all the doctors and nurses there would love to have all of us boys running up and down the halls, making noise and disturbing the patients." All of the boys laughed; the image was really very funny.

Thankfully, Sabatino's aim soon improved and no one was

injured. After about an hour, it was time for dinner. As they headed inside, Gavriel thought of what Mercado had just said, about the boys going to visit Rachamim in the hospital. And then it occurred to him – the hospital! One of the British military hospitals! Of course, this was so obvious. Why hadn't he thought of this sooner?

For the first time in weeks, Gavriel had a new plan! There were many military hospitals throughout the city operated by the various allies. A very large British one was situated not that far away from the orphanage. Here, Gavriel was certain, there was no sentry on guard, and it would probably be easy to get into the building. Once inside, he could try to sell a few newspapers and meet some of the soldiers. These soldiers would be recuperating from their injuries, not hurrying along the street. Gavriel would probably be able to talk to them and even engage them in conversation.

Immediately after school the very next day, Daniel set out for the British military hospital. Just as he had done on that failed trip to Camp Summerhill, he carried his kaleidoscope and a bag of newspapers with him. This time, fortunately, he did not have as far to walk, and within a few short minutes, he soon reached his destination.

As he bounded up the small dirt path that led to the main entrance, Gavriel had a strong sense that there was somebody, somewhere in the hospital, who was going to be able to help him.

Gavriel was right.

*Salonika
May 1917*

**D**aniel opened his eyes again, this time forcing himself to keep them open a little bit longer. He had opened his eyes many times before, but exhaustion had always overtaken him and he had closed them in a matter of seconds. Now he was feeling a bit stronger, and he slowly started to look around. He knew he was in an unfamiliar place, but he had no idea where he was or who had brought him here.

He thought he heard someone at his right side. He tried unsuccesfully to turn his head in that direction, but his head felt heavy, as if it were held down by weights. He tried a second time, but it was impossible.

"Now don't strain yourself, Danny," said an unfamiliar, accented voice emanating from somewhere nearby. "You've had a nasty bit of business. You scared the living daylights out of everyone here, you did."

Daniel had no idea where this voice was coming from. Daniel shifted his gaze, and to his surprise, he thought he discerned the figure of an enormous, dark-haired man sitting

CHAPTER TWENTY-FIVE

on the bed to his left. The man appeared to be dressed in an army issue shirt and a … a what? A skirt? *Oh, my*, Daniel thought to himself, *I must be very ill. I must be hallucinating.*

"How are you feeling, Danny? My name is Duncan McPhee and I have been in the bed beside you for the past three weeks. Yes, that's right, three weeks. You have had it bad, my friend, real bad. You were already here when they brought me in, and I can tell you, they thought you were about to give up the ghost, they did. But somehow you held on." Daniel tried to talk, but all that came out of his mouth was a groan.

"I will tell you all about it. You see, I've been listening to these nurses for weeks now. You know, I'm bored, lying around here, waiting for my leg to heal, and everyone keeps talking about what a sight you were when they brought you in.

That's right, a real sight. I think it was that young Canadian medic, Lester Pearson, who brought you in. The story is that they found you collapsed in your tent at Summerhill Camp. Turns out you had pneumonia, double pneumonia, if you can believe it – both lungs!"

Daniel was trying to absorb everything this … this apparition was telling him. He looked more closely at him and then he started to understand. The accent, the skirt—the soldier was Scottish! The soldier was wearing a kilt, part of the uniform of the Argyll and Sutherland Highlanders.

"Anyway, Danny, I hope you don't mind if I call you Danny, I heard the nurses say your first name is Daniel. Anyway, I'm here because a whizzbang took a piece out of my left leg. They had to operate, but they tell me it will be almost as good as new by the time I go home. I'm feeling much better, except at night when the pain is pretty bad. Well, as I always say, it could have been worse, could have been worse."

Daniel really wanted to talk to the soldier; he had a lot of questions to ask him. He tried to clear his throat. He wanted to ask Duncan where he was and whether anyone had contacted his parents to let them know he was ill ….

Daniel heard the soft, hurried footsteps of someone approaching. Duncan called in the direction of the sound, "Nurse, nurse! Danny's eyes are open, and he's focusing on everything I say. I can tell, he looks alert. This is the first time I have ever seen him like this."

A young woman, dressed in the long grey dress, white apron and small white cap of a British army nurse, hurried over to Daniel's bedside. *I am in a British military hospital*, Daniel thought to himself.

The nurse looked closely at Daniel and said cheerfully, "Private Sheinfeld, good morning! How are you feeling?"

In a weak voice, Daniel replied, "I am not sure."

"Now, Private Sheinfeld, do not try too hard to talk. You have been very ill and you have had an extremely high fever for weeks. It appears that your fever has finally broken, and hopefully, you are now on the road to recovery. But, please, you must be careful not to exert yourself. I will check on you in an hour. If you need anything, I am sure Private McPhee here will be willing to help you." And with that, she walked away to tend to another patient in the room.

"That's Nurse Merriweather, who's been looking after me and you ever since we got here," explained Duncan. "You heard what she said. Anything, anything at all, just ask me. Of course, I can't do too much running around right now, on account of my bad leg, but I am sure I can help you with almost everything else." Duncan smiled at Daniel.

Daniel said, very slowly, "Is my kitbag here?"

"Yes, it sure is, right over by the side here." Duncan went over to retrieve it and put it on Daniel's bed. "What do you need? Let me get it for you." Daniel wondered how he was going to explain to this Scottish soldier that he needed his *siddur*, his *yarmulke* and his *tallis katan*.

"Inside, I have a small book of Hebrew prayers, and a small cap, and, I think, a thin white shirt, it is trimmed with strings, it is …"

"Let me see. Yes, here you are. I think this is the little book you want," said Duncan as he rummaged through Daniel's kitbag. "Now, a little cap, *hmm*, oh, is this it?" Daniel nodded. "And a little shirt with strings, well, let me check here at the bottom …" In a second or two, he pulled out Daniel's *tallis katan*. He handed all three items to Daniel.

By now, Daniel had managed to prop himself up. He slowly put the *yarmulke* on his head and tentatively took the *siddur* in his right hand. He looked at the *tallis katan* sadly – he didn't think he had the strength to pull it over his head. Both he and Duncan stared at it for a minute.

"You know, Danny, it's a funny thing. I am not sure what

that is, that clothing there with the strings, but it reminds me of someone. Just about a week ago, I met a little Greek boy around here. I've heard he comes around selling newspapers every few days. Cute boy, very sweet. I always buy a paper from him, even though they give them out here for free. Well, anyway, every time I see him, he seems to have these same kind of strings hanging out of his trousers. I have never seen anything like this before. I thought it was something Greek boys wore. But now I see you have them too, and you're British. If you don't mind me asking, what are those things?"

Daniel's heart skipped a beat. What had Duncan just said? A little boy with *tzitzis* was coming around to the hospital and selling newspapers? Ignoring Duncan's question for a minute, Daniel asked, "A little boy? Recently? Who is he?"

"Oh, I don't know, he looks poor, you know, beaten up shoes, old clothes, but a nice boy, really polite. Has an interest in ships, of all things. Anyway, what are those strings?"

"I think that the newspaper boy is Jewish, as am I. We both wear these because it is part of a biblical commandment that tells us to attach fringes to every four-cornered garment that we wear."

"Very interesting," said Duncan. "You wear special clothes. Reminds me a bit of us Scots. You know, we also have our own special clothes, our kilts."

"When is the boy coming back?" asked Daniel.

"Oh, I don't know, maybe today, maybe tomorrow. But if it's a newspaper you're after, I am sure we could ask one of the nurses to bring you one," Duncan answered amiably.

"No, I want to meet the boy."

"You want to meet him? Why? Do you know him?" asked Duncan.

"No, no, I want to ask with something."

"Well, it's a bit of a strange request," replied Duncan. "But Danny, you've been so sick, if this will make you feel better, I'm happy to help."

# CHAPTER TWENTY-SIX

"**D**anny, Danny, here's the newspaper boy I was telling you about," Duncan announced a few days later as he walked into the hospital ward.

Daniel, now dressed in his uniform, was out of bed and dozing on a chair. He opened his eyes and was greeted by the sight of a little boy. The boy appeared to be around eleven years old. He had thick black hair, a dark complexion and large, lively brown eyes. He was dressed in a short cotton shirt, an old cloth cap, short trousers and just as Duncan had said – *tzitzis* hanging out of both sides of his trousers.

Gavriel looked at Daniel – at this tall, blonde, gaunt British soldier. He could not imagine why in the world this soldier had wanted to see him, yet the Scottish soldier had said that there was another soldier at the hospital who was anxious to meet him.

Daniel did not know what language the young boy spoke. He held out his hand and said, in an almost questioning tone, "*Shalom aleichem?*"

Gavriel's eyes lit up with immediate

comprehension. He shook Daniel's hand and replied, "*Aleichem shalom!*"

To Gavriel's and Duncan's surprise, Daniel's eyes immediately filled with tears. He quickly wiped them away with the back of his hand and asked Duncan, "How do you communicate with the boy? Do you speak Greek?"

Before Duncan could answer, Gavriel said excitedly, "No, sir, I speak English! And I am very pleased to meet you."

"I am pleased to meet you, as well. My name is Daniel Sheinfeld. What is your name?" Daniel inquired.

Gavriel replied, in almost unaccented English, "My name is Gavriel Florentin."

"Where are you from, Gavriel?" asked Daniel.

"I am from Salonika, but I have an aunt and an uncle in Leeds, in Leeds, England."

"How interesting," said Daniel. "And you live with your parents, here in Salonika?" Daniel asked.

"No, my parents, of blessed memory, are no longer alive," answered Gavriel.

"Oh, my goodness, you poor boy, you are an orphan!" exclaimed Duncan, who was following the conversation with tremendous interest.

"Where do you live?" Daniel asked.

"I live at the Allatini Orphanage for Jewish Boys."

"And where is that?" asked Daniel.

"Oh, it's not that far from here. It's just a few blocks away."

Daniel asked, "Are there any Jewish shops or perhaps a synagogue in the city?"

"Oh, yes," replied Gavriel. "There are many synagogues in Salonika, and the streets near the Via Egnata are full of stores where you can buy ..."

Duncan began to feel completely left out of the conversation. Amazingly, it seemed that although these two Jews had never met before, they had an enormous amount to talk about. He excused himself from the conversation and went to play cards with some of the other soldiers in the room.

Daniel and Gavriel talked for quite a while. After about half an hour, Gavriel noticed that Daniel was looking increasingly tired, and he sensed that Daniel needed to rest. Gavriel decided that today was not the right day to ask the soldier about ships bound for England. Really, he could wait another day or two; he had already waited so long, one more day or so would not make a difference.

Instead, he said to Daniel, "I must return to the orphanage now. Maybe I will come back and visit you in a few days' time."

Daniel nodded and said, "Yes, I would like that." Gavriel said good-bye and told Daniel that he would try to come back soon.

As Daniel watched Gavriel leave, he realized that the boy would probably be able to help him navigate the Jewish part of the city. Surprisingly, the fact that there was a Jewish community existent in Salonika did not make Daniel happy. All he felt was a dull sense of relief, but nothing more than that. Just the thought of walking in the city was exhausting.

Daniel knew full well, having been told at length by both

Duncan and the nurses, that he had been extremely ill. He had spent many weeks in bed, delirious at times with a raging fever. There had been little anyone could do other than give him fluids and aspirin and hope that his body was somehow strong enough to shake off the infection that had seized hold of both of his lungs.

Daniel had begun to recover physically, and every day he felt slightly stronger than the day before. Yet, Daniel was overwhelmed by a sense of despondency. From the moment he awoke in the morning until the time he said *Shema* at night, Daniel felt weary, listless and not at all like his usual easygoing, level-headed self.

In addition, Daniel was haunted by the feeling that he had failed his friends by not being with them on the Western Front.

Rationally, he knew that this had not been his fault, but in his distorted frame of mind, Daniel felt somehow responsible. Over and over again, Daniel said to himself – "If only I had been with them, if only I could have looked out for Chezki, if only I had been with Moishe, talking to him, reassuring him, if only I would have been with Avrumi … I could have helped him … if only …"

After Gavriel had left, Daniel remained seated in the chair. He wanted to lie down but did not have the energy to return to his bed. Instead, he dozed off in the chair again, the words "if only … if only …" reverberating in his mind.

*Salonika*
*May/June 1917*

# CHAPTER TWENTY-SEVEN

Gavriel began to visit Daniel a few times a week in the afternoon, after lunch. Gavriel's friend Yona had become increasingly curious about where Gavriel was going.

One morning on their way to the Talmud Torah, Yona said to Gavriel, "So, when is the ship leaving?"

"What do you mean? What ship?" asked Gavriel.

"The ship that will take you to England, of course," replied Yona.

"Oh, I don't know about any ships. I haven't found out yet," Gavriel replied matter-of-factly.

"You haven't found out yet?" Yona repeated, sounding surprised. "Then why have you been so busy in the afternoons, these past few weeks? I thought you were making plans for your trip," Yona added.

Gavriel explained to Yona that he had met a British soldier, a Jewish soldier, in fact, who was convalescing in the British military hospital not that far from the orphanage. He told Yona that the soldier, who looked very young, maybe only just a few years older than they were, had been seriously ill for a number of weeks. He explained to him that the soldier, who was from London and whose name was Daniel, was just now starting to recover.

"So you mean you haven't even asked him yet if he knows about any ships?" Yona asked, incredulous.

"No, not yet. You see, Yona, Daniel is alone here in Salonika, without any friends or family." Realizing that Daniel did indeed have one friend, that funny Scottish soldier who seemed to have taken Daniel under his wing, Gavriel corrected himself, "Well, actually, he does have one friend, another soldier, who is very nice, but that soldier is not from Salonika, and he is not Jewish, which means that he can't really help him the way that I can. You know, tell him where the synagogues are, where to buy kosher food, things like that."

Yona thought about this for a minute. The reality of Gavriel's selflessness slowly began to penetrate. Yona did not know what to say. He had always known that Gavriel was special. Yona was simply in awe of his friend.

Every time Gavriel visited, he would tell Daniel a little bit more about himself – stories about his late mother, memories of his life at the Benvenistes and details about living in the orphanage. Daniel, by contrast, said very little. He did once reveal to Gavriel the fact that immediately before he became ill, he had received some very bad news about his friends on the Western Front, but Gavriel could tell from the look on Daniel's face that he did not want to discuss it.

Gavriel knew from Duncan that Daniel had been critically ill for weeks, and Gavriel could see that Daniel was still quite weak. Gavriel sensed that the Daniel he had met in the hospital bore little resemblance to the Daniel who had originally enlisted in the army, and he also correctly sensed that Daniel's weakness was not purely physical in nature.

Gavriel was more than happy to help Daniel in any way possible, and he kept telling Daniel that as soon as he was strong enough, they would go for a walk together in the city and Gavriel would show him some of the areas of Jewish interest.

After a number of weeks, Daniel appeared to have gained some weight and his color had improved. Daniel was able to walk around the hospital a little bit, and he was encouraged to go outside as much as possible. The nurses hoped that the fresh air would strengthen Daniel's lungs.

In early June, after consulting with the doctor, the nurses told Daniel that he was allowed to leave the hospital for a short time.

The first thing Daniel wanted to do was replace his lost *tefillin*. He asked Gavriel to take him to the nearest *sofer* and Gavriel gladly obliged.

One Sunday afternoon, with Duncan looking on nervously, Daniel and Gavriel set out for the *sofer*. As they left the hospital, Duncan called after them, "Make sure Danny doesn't walk too fast. Make sure he rests every few minutes. Make sure Danny doesn't exert himself."

Gavriel laughed and called back to Duncan, "Don't worry, we will walk very slowly."

Gavriel led Daniel through a number of short, interconnected streets and alleyways. Gavriel always enjoyed walking along the streets of Salonika; he enjoyed the sweet fragrance of the roses in bloom and the sight of the lush fruit trees, their branches heavy with figs and apricots slowly ripening in the summer sun.

Daniel, by contrast, was only vaguely aware of his surroundings. All of the streets of the city looked the same to him – narrow, dark and ancient.

In a few minutes, the two of them reached the *sofer*. With Gavriel acting as translator, Daniel was able to purchase new *tefillin* and a small cloth bag. Gavriel was happy for Daniel, but he sensed that the transaction had distressed Daniel. In fact, as Daniel paid the *sofer*, Gavriel noticed that Daniel's hands shook and that he seemed to have difficulty catching his breath.

Gavriel was right; Daniel had indeed found the experience upsetting. Although he was relieved to have *tefillin* again, as soon as he held it in his hands, the words of Avrumi's letter returned to haunt him, "I gathered Chezki's personal effects to be sent home – his *siddur* and *tefillin*, the letters and photos his family had sent him ..."

Gavriel, noticing now that Daniel was looking extremely pale, ushered him outside, hoping that the fresh air would revive him. He quickly found him an empty seat at one of the outdoor cafes. And then, thinking that perhaps Daniel needed a few minutes alone, he told him he going to look at something in one of the shops and that he would return in a few minutes.

Daniel, still holding the *tefillin*, slumped down in his chair. Preoccupied with his painful memories, he did not notice the approach of a heavy-set middle-aged man with a large handlebar moustache.

"*Reb Yid*," said the man, startling Daniel, "*vos tut a Yiddishe bachur in dem ort, fun alle erter* (what is a Jewish boy doing here, of all places)?" Daniel was momentarily taken aback; how did the man know he was Jewish? Then he realized that the man must have noticed his *tefillin* bag. Daniel answered in Yiddish, the language he had learned at home and the language his parents still used when they spoke to each other.

"*Ich bin a privat in de Englishe arme, und zei hubben mir geshikt da tsu Salonika*. (I am a private in the British army, and I am stationed here in Salonika.)"

The man introduced himself as Getsel Kroit and told Daniel that he was originally from Warsaw, but that business interests had taken him and his family to Salonika. Daniel nodded politely, but was not that interested in what the man was saying. Daniel was upset and tired, and wanted to go back to the hospital.

The man then said, "*Vult ir gevelt kummen tsu mir und mein mishpacha oif Shabbos, dem Freitik bar nacht far mitug* (Would you like to join me and my family this *Shabbos*, this Friday night for dinner)?" Daniel felt much too tired to contemplate such an invitation, and he almost declined. But then he thought of the boy, of Gavriel – Gavriel, an orphan who had probably not had a *Shabbos* meal with a family in close to a year.

"*A sheinem dank, Reb Yid, dos iz zeyer freintlich fun eich. Vult ich efsher kennen brengen a freint mit mir* (Thank you, sir, that is most kind of you. Would you mind, could I possibly bring a friend with me)?" he asked.

"*Avada! Ir zult beide kummen tsu mein hoiz Freitik nuch Maariv* (Why certainly! Both of you should come to my house Friday night, right after *Maariv*)," replied Mr. Kroit. He then gave Daniel his address.

Gavriel joined Daniel a few minutes later. Daniel told Gavriel about the invitation, and from the smile that lit up Gavriel's face, Daniel could see that the boy was very excited about the idea. *Well*, Daniel thought to himself, *maybe Gavriel will have enough enthusiasm for both of us.*

**M**r. Capon readily gave Gavriel permission to have dinner with the Kroit family. He knew that Gavriel was a responsible boy who would stay out of trouble, and he knew he could trust him to return before it got too late.

Within hours, it seemed, everyone in the orphanage had heard about Gavriel's invitation. Such invitations were rarely, if ever, extended to the boys. Most of them ate every single meal at the institution, three times a day, seven days a week, from the day that they were left there until the day that they were considered old enough to leave and fend for themselves.

Yona was very excited for Gavriel. Despite Gavriel's protests, he was adamant that Gavriel borrow his nice white shirt. Before Gavriel left, he also insisted that Gavriel brush his hair not once, but twice, to make sure he looked presentable for the Kroit family.

As they had arranged, Daniel and Gavriel met each other after *Maariv* outside the Mosca Synagogue, the main Ashkenazi synagogue in Salonika.

With Gavriel leading the way, they headed

south toward the port, and then east near the shoreline on Vassilisis Street, where a number of villas and mansions had recently been built. As they walked, Gavriel noticed that Daniel was walking at a fairly rapid pace, and not once did he need to slow down to catch his breath.

Within twenty minutes, they came to the large, stately home of Mr. Getsel Kroit. Daniel pushed open the heavy wrought iron gate that closed the house off from the street, and he and Gavriel walked up the long smoothly paved path. When they reached the entrance to the house, Daniel knocked on the thick wooden door.

After a minute, a young woman wearing the starched, pressed black uniform of a European maid opened the door. The maid looked at Daniel in his uniform and nodded, as if to confirm that he was, indeed, whom she had been told to expect. She said, "Please come in."

She then looked at Gavriel. Her face registered surprise, but she had been trained to keep her opinions to herself, so she simply said, "Please follow me to the drawing room. Mr. Kroit has not come home yet, but Mrs. Kroit is waiting for you there."

The maid led Daniel into the room and Gavriel followed. Seated on a large overstuffed chesterfield was a middle-aged woman dressed in a long, velvet gown. The woman stood up as soon as she saw Daniel enter the room.

She glided over to him and said in Yiddish, in a voice thick with pretension, "You must be the British soldier my husband told me about. My name is Gruna Kroit. I am so very pleased to meet you." Nodding in the direction of two young women sitting stiffly on two nearby chairs, she continued, "These two lovely young ladies are my daughters. Their names are –"

Just as she was about to introduce them, she suddenly spotted Gavriel standing behind Daniel. In a second, the expression on her face changed from one of well-rehearsed poise to one of complete alarm. She bellowed, "Zlata, Zlata, who is this boy? How did he get into my house?"

Without waiting for the maid to reply, Mrs. Kroit turned back to Daniel and said in a considerably more refined tone of voice, "Is your friend, the other soldier, is he meeting you here at our house?"

Realizing what had happened, Daniel pointed to Gavriel and said, "My friend is right here, Mrs. Kroit. Allow me to introduce you to Gavriel Florentin."

Gavriel, who did not know Yiddish and had not followed any of the conversation, nodded politely at the mention of his name and said *Shabbat Shalom.*

The woman looked directly at Gavriel now and sniffed the air as if she were detecting an unpleasant smell. She then turned to Daniel and said, "I am sorry. I do not understand. This little, little boy, he is your friend? This is my other guest? This is who my husband invited? There must be some mistake."

At that very moment, Mr. Kroit entered the drawing room. "Good *Shabbos,* everyone," he said. Noticing the pained look on his wife's face, he said, "What is wrong, Gruna?" The woman was barely able to contain herself.

Pointing directly at Gavriel, she said loudly, in a Yiddish so rapid that Daniel had trouble following it, "Getsel, you told me that two Jewish soldiers were coming for dinner. You said *two* soldiers, not one soldier and a little boy, a dirty, unkempt little boy! I cannot have this, this, street urchin, here, in my beautiful, elegant home! What will the neighbors say? *Oy! Oy!* I am ruined, completely ruined!"

Despite the language barrier, Gavriel by now had a pretty clear understanding of what had happened. He said quietly to Daniel, "I don't think the woman was expecting me. I think it is better that I leave and go back to the orphanage right now. This woman does not want me here. But, Daniel, you stay. They were expecting you."

Daniel shook his head vigorously. "No," he said to Gavriel. "I will not stay here without you."

Then, drawing himself up to his full height and clearing his throat loudly, Daniel said, "There seems to have been a misunderstanding. I believe, Mr. Kroit, that your wife was expecting two young men this evening. Under the circumstances, I think it best that we leave now."

"Leave? Leave? No, no, absolutely not! Please, my wife was just confused. Please, stay, stay and have dinner with us," Getsel Kroit pleaded.

"No, sir, I am sorry, but we are leaving now," Daniel declared.

Without saying another word, Daniel purposefully left the drawing room, strode into the hallway, opened one of the large front doors forcefully, and promptly left the house. Gavriel followed closely behind.

Once outside, the two of them looked at each other in astonishment. "Can you believe what just happened?" asked Daniel. "I have never experienced anything so rude in my life!" he exclaimed.

"Oh, Daniel, you didn't have to leave because of me! You should have stayed. They probably had all kinds of food that you are used to from home, things that you would enjoy, like *gefilterra* fish and *knaidlerosos.*"

Daniel immediately broke into laughter at Gavriel's unintentionally hilarious pronunciation of the Yiddish words. "*Gefilterra fish? Knaidlerosos?* I am sorry to disappoint you, Gavriel, but my mother never served any of those." Daniel continued to laugh, his lopsided smile evident for the first time in many months.

Daniel and Gavriel began to walk back in the direction they had so recently come from. When they reached the orphanage, Daniel said, "Gavriel, I am so sorry about what happened this evening. I had no idea that they were expecting two soldiers."

"Please don't apologize. It wasn't your fault." Gavriel then wished Daniel a *Shabbat Shalom* and went inside.

All eyes were upon Gavriel as he entered the dining room a few minutes later. No one had expected him for a few more hours. Yona approached him immediately and said, his voice full of concern, "Why are you home so early? Did something bad happen?"

Remembering the way Daniel stood tall and proud in the Kroits' drawing room, his forceful stride out of the house and his laughter at Gavriel's inability to pronounce Yiddish, Gavriel replied with a smile, "No, Yona, not at all. Something very good happened this evening."

D aniel felt terrible about the way that Gavriel had been treated at the Kroits' house. He was shocked that people could have such brazen disregard for someone else's feelings – especially the feelings of a child! They had embarrassed the poor boy, on *Shabbos*, of all days!

Growing up, Daniel's parents had always stressed the value of never embarrassing anyone. He and his sisters had been taught from an early age that if a customer were ever to come into the shop, ask for a few items and then discover that he did not, in fact, have enough money, they, the Sheinfeld children, were to tell the customer not to worry, that the balance could be paid at a later time. And, of course, the children had been instructed to never ask the customer for the money the next time they saw him.

Daniel decided that he wanted to do something nice for Gavriel, to surprise him. He had no idea what that might be. Daniel knew the perfect person to talk to – Duncan! Duncan was a wonderful source of information, and

Duncan was very fond of "the little newspaper boy," as he called him. And so, one morning after breakfast, Daniel asked him if he could think of something nice to do for Gavriel.

Duncan didn't even have to think for a minute. He answered immediately, "Take him to the White Tower."

"You mean that huge tower that overlooks the city from the shore?"

"Yes, sir, that's the one. I doubt the little newspaper boy has ever had a chance to go, and it is a sight to be seen. Once, when I was on leave about six months ago, before I was injured, I climbed up there with two of my buddies. You get a great view from the top, and once you're up there, there is a little restaurant where you can get drinks and snacks."

Suddenly remembering Daniel's need for kosher food, he added, "I am sure there is something the two of you could eat there." Then Duncan paused for a minute. "But you know, Danny, it is rather a steep climb. Do you think you are up for it?" Daniel smiled at Duncan; sometimes the big Scottish soldier reminded him of a giant clucking mother hen.

"Yes, I think I can manage it," Daniel reassured him.

The next day, Daniel and Gavriel set out for the White Tower. Duncan had been right. Gavriel had never been there before and had always wanted to go to this landmark that towered above the city. He brought his kaleidoscope with him, telling Daniel that he often took it with him when he walked the city streets.

The large tower loomed thirty-five meters tall and commanded the eastern end of the port, its presence dominating the shoreline. It had been built by the Turks in the fifteenth century and had originally been used as a prison. The rounded stone edifice bore the marks of many previous battles and numerous small windows had been painstakingly cut out of its thick stone walls.

Gavriel and Daniel entered the tower and began the long and arduous climb to the top. The huge stone stairs were high and uneven and wound steeply around the interior of the building.

Duncan had been right. It was indeed a steep climb, with neither ramps nor handrails to ease their ascent. When they reached the top Daniel needed to rest. He and Gavriel went into the small restaurant and Daniel bought two *limonadas*. After a few minutes, they went to look at the view.

Gavriel and Daniel gazed in amazement at the immense mountains far away in the distance, the dark blue waters of the Aegean Sea below and the ancient buildings and multi-colored houses all around them. Neither of them had ever seen anything so spectacular before. After a few minutes, Gavriel retrieved his kaleidoscope from his pocket and held it up to the luminous summer sun.

Noticing the kaleidoscope, Daniel said, "You know, Gavriel, that toy of yours reminds me of what I was trained to do in the army." Gavriel put the kaleidoscope down and turned to face Daniel. This sounded very interesting. Daniel had never told him what he had done in the army.

"I was trained as a signaler, that is, I was trained to use something called a heliograph. And the heliograph, from the first moment I saw it, reminded me of a kaleidoscope."

"What does it do?' asked Gavriel.

"Well, light bounces off a mirror embedded inside, much like it does in the kaleidoscope. The only difference is there aren't any colorful pieces inside so you can't see combinations of colors and shapes, like you do. All you see is the light reflected off of the mirror."

"Daniel, if you don't mind my saying so, the two really aren't that similar. You said yourself that the heliograph only reflects light. It is basically a tool. But the kaleidoscope, really, is much better."

"What do you mean it is better? Yours is a simple toy, whereas the heliograph is an accurate, effective signaling device," Daniel said, intrigued.

"Well, you see, Daniel, the kaleidoscope allows me to see images and colors in different ways. I can see purples and blues today when I hold it one way, and tomorrow, I can see reds and pinks if I hold it another way. I can shake it up and see only green, and sometimes I see just yellow."

"Gavriel, that's very nice, but it is still just a toy," said Daniel.

"No, Daniel, for me it is much more than that." Daniel looked puzzled as Gavriel continued. "The kaleidoscope reminds me of my mother, of the way she taught me to see the world. Because, you know, everything can be seen in a variety of different ways."

Daniel looked intently at Gavriel. "Gavriel, I know you are just a child, but how can you possibly think there are different ways to see everything? Some things are just ... horrible ... tragic ... What about ... about illness ... about ..."

Daniel did not have to continue. Gavriel knew what Daniel meant. He remembered Daniel telling him once that he had received very upsetting news about his friends on the Western Front.

"Daniel, the way my mother explained it to me was that everything depends on how you look at things. Although to us, something may seem difficult, or even terrible, everything is from *Senor del Mundo*, and everything has a purpose, a reason. It is just that we, at that moment, may not be able to see it. Later on, at another time, we may be able to see the reason and understand why something has happened."

Daniel was silent, stunned. Gavriel's words penetrated him deeply. He was impressed by Gavriel's ability to express himself so clearly in English, but, much more than that, he was amazed by Gavriel's wisdom. Was Gavriel right? Would there come a day when Daniel would be able to see all that he had been through in the past year in a different light?

As the two of them began to descend from the tower, winding their way around and around the huge circular stairs, Gavriel's words echoed over and over again in Daniel's mind.

**D**uncan hurried outside. Looking around the courtyard of the hospital, he bellowed, "Danny, Danny! Where are you? I have the most exciting news."

"Over here, Duncan," Daniel called from where he sat underneath a large almond tree. Duncan came over to Daniel and took a seat beside him.

"Danny, you won't believe what I overheard Nurse Merriweather saying, just now, as I was walking in the hall."

"Overheard?" Daniel asked.

"Oh, Danny, she was talking so loudly to another nurse, I couldn't help myself," replied Duncan with a sheepish grin on his broad face.

"Duncan, when you listen so attentively, you can't fail to overhear," Daniel remarked, smiling at his big friend.

"Listen, Danny, this is what she said. She said both of us are now well enough to be discharged from the hospital! She said that because of our medical problems – me with my bad leg and you with your bad lungs – the brass has decided that we are unfit for further service.

# CHAPTER THIRTY

We are getting discharged! We are being sent home!"

Daniel's eyes widened in surprise. "And Danny, she said that arrangements are being made for both of us to sail by the end of this coming week!"

Daniel couldn't believe what Duncan had just told him. He was going home! *Baruch Hashem*, he was going home! "Duncan, this is great news! I can't believe this! I must write my parents a letter right away and tell them! Duncan, thank you so much! Thank you for telling me!"

Daniel immediately went back to his room and grabbed his kitbag. As he searched for a pen and paper, he suddenly realized something; he was going to have to say good-bye to Gavriel.

Daniel was tremendously appreciative of everything the boy had done for him. For months now, Gavriel had visited him several times a week. He had taken him to the synagogue and helped him buy *tefillin* and kosher food.

But, most importantly, Daniel now realized, Gavriel had helped him recover, not just physically but in a deeper, more profound way. Gavriel had taught Daniel a very important lesson that day at the White Tower. He had taught him about the importance of perspective.

Daniel wanted to show Gavriel his appreciation, but he did not know what the boy would like. Gavriel always seemed so amazingly self-sufficient. He never complained and never asked for anything. *But there must be something he would like*, Daniel thought. *There just had to be something.*

Gavriel was thrilled for Daniel when heard the news later the next day. "*Gracias al Dio* (Thank *Hashem*)! That is wonderful!" he enthused.

Smiling broadly in anticipation Daniel replied, "I am so happy! I can't wait to see my parents, my sisters, my friends." Daniel continued, "Gavriel, I've been thinking. Since I am going to be leaving soon, I would like to get you something. You know, to thank you for everything you've done for me."

Gavriel replied, "No, no, Daniel, it isn't necessary. I don't need anything. I am just happy that you are finally going home."

Daniel insisted, "Gavriel, please, there must be something you really want, something important that I could get for you, something you can't get for yourself."

Gavriel paused for a minute and then said, "Well, Daniel there is something, actually, that I want very badly, but I don't think it is what you had in mind."

"Tell me! Gavriel, you must tell me! I want to hear about it," Daniel entreated.

For the next fifteen minutes, Gavriel told Daniel everything that had happened to him over the past few months – how the Benvenistes had moved, how he had been left at the orphanage, how Mrs. Habib had promised that it was only for a little while, how Mr. Capon seemed reluctant to send him to his aunt and uncle in England, how Gavriel had become tired of waiting and decided that he would try to arrange things on his own, and how he had made various attempts, up until his meeting with Daniel.

Daniel's eyes were riveted on Gavriel's face as Gavriel told him his story. He was deeply touched that during the entire time that he had known him, Gavriel had not once asked for his help. He understood that Gavriel had sacrificed his own needs for him, for Daniel.

There was one part of the story that just didn't make sense to Daniel. Why hadn't Mr. Capon sent the boy to England already? It was true that initially, when Gavriel had first arrived at the orphanage, civilian travel had been prohibited. But now, the seas were relatively quiet and a number of civilian ships did leave the port. Gavriel told Daniel that after the humiliating experience with the soldiers on the Via Egnata, Mr. Capon had told him that there were other, "more complex" reasons that Gavriel could not travel. But what were they?

Daniel had a strong feeling that part of the story was missing.

"Gavriel, I am going to do my best to try to arrange this for you. I don't know how yet, but hopefully, *bli neder*, early next week before I leave, I will go and speak to Mr. Capon. I want to hear the whole story from him and see how quickly we can arrange a ticket for you to sail to England."

Gavriel was speechless. Finally, finally, after all of these long months of waiting, things were starting to happen!

G avriel was sitting outside the orphanage on a small wicker bench. Although many of the boys in the orphanage had gone back to their rooms after lunch to take a short *Shabbos* nap, Gavriel was too excited to sleep.

He kept thinking about what Daniel had said to him the other day – that he was going to speak to Mr. Capon early in the coming week, and that he was going to try to arrange for him to go to England. Gavriel had been waiting for this for so long, he could hardly believe that it was finally going to happen.

Gavriel noticed a stocky, broad-shouldered figure coming toward him. Gavriel soon realized that it was Sebi, and he cringed. Gavriel had always tried to avoid Sebi as much as possible, but unfortunately, Sebi now walked right up to him and planted himself directly in front of Gavriel.

"So, Gavriel, how are your plans going?" he asked.

"Everything is fine, Sebi," replied Gavriel.

# CHAPTER THIRTY-ONE

"Has your friend the Jewish soldier helped you yet?" Sebi asked, the hint of a sardonic smile playing on his face.

Gavriel did not know how Sebi knew about Daniel, but he did not want to prolong the conversation by asking. He merely answered, "I hope so."

"Really, is that a fact? The soldier is going to help you. Why do I find that hard to believe? A total stranger, not even from Salonika, is going to help you get to England. *Hmm.*"

Sebi paused as if pretending to think this over. Gavriel did not say anything. He was hoping Sebi would soon lose interest in this conversation if Gavriel remained quiet, and that he would soon just walk away.

"A total stranger, a British soldier, is helping little Gavriel Florentin. Really? No, Gavriel, I think you have it all wrong. Seems to me, you are the one who has been doing all the helping. Yes, it seems to me the soldier found himself a very reliable errand boy. Someone to take him around, get him things. Yes, that's how it seems to me."

Gavriel knew that he mustn't let Sebi see how much his words offended him. In a calm voice he simply said, "No, Sebi, I think the soldier is really going to help me."

Sebi virtually snorted. "Sure, Gavriel, go ahead and believe him if you want. Be a fool. But I, *I* know how these things work." Sebi continued, his voice getting louder and more insistent. "I know the way adults are. They'll say anything to children. Just think about it. Look at that old lady, whatever her name was, the one who left you here. I bet she told you that you would be here only for a short time. Right? Hah!

"And what about Mr. Capon, what did he say to you?" Then, in an attempt to imitate the director, Sebi's loud voice became soft and reassuring. "Don't worry, Gavriel, I will put you on a ship for England soon; don't worry, the ship is coming soon, don't worry –"

"Sebi, you're not right," Gavriel interjected, finding it increasingly difficult to keep silent. "Adults don't lie. But sometimes things happen, things change and they can't …"

Sebi ignored Gavriel and continued. "Oh, and Gavriel, what about the biggest liars of all, your precious aunt and uncle in England? Sure, they love you, but that doesn't mean that they would actually want you to go and live with them."

Unable to control himself now, Gavriel snapped, "Sebi, that is not true! That is just not true! My aunt and uncle do want me. Mrs. Habib told me so. It's just that it wasn't safe to travel and I had to wait a little bit and then …"

"Gavriel, you are a fool. There have been civilian ships sailing from here for months. I've been down at the port, and I've seen all sorts of people getting onto ships. Don't you understand? You can't go to England because your aunt and uncle have forgotten all about you."

Gavriel felt a surge of anger, an emotion that was strange to him. In a voice that did not sound familiar to his own ears, he looked straight into Sebi's menacing face.

"Everything you have just said is completely untrue. You are a liar." Then he turned his back toward him and started to walk away.

Sebi quickly followed after him. "A liar, a liar? You call *me* a liar? I am not the liar. It is all of them. Adults, they are the liars." Gavriel picked up his pace. He had to get away from Sebi, from these horrible, hateful words.

Sebi ran after him screeching, "Liars, liars, they are all liars. All of them, just like my own mother … Liars, liars, all of them!"

Gavriel put his hands over his ears. He started to run. He ran and ran and ran. He did not stop running until he got to a place where he felt safe.

D uncan and Daniel were seated outside in the courtyard. Duncan was telling Daniel all about various members of his family back home in Inverary, a city in the northwest part of Scotland.

"And then there's my older sister, Fiona, and her husband Harry. Harry is a grocer, and they have four children, girls all of them, the cutest little things. The first one, Cora, she's eight, and then there's ..."

Daniel was listening, but only half-heartedly. Since learning that they were scheduled to depart from Salonika later this week, Duncan had decided that it was imperative that Daniel learn the names, ages and life stories of all the members of the McPhee family. And, as it turned out, Duncan had a huge family.

As Daniel's mind began to wander, he shifted his gaze away from Duncan. He looked up at the sky and suddenly noticed a large dark cloud in the west. How unusual, he thought to himself. The sky was a beautiful clear blue, yet there was one large rain cloud poised to descend. Was it a really a rain cloud or could it possibly be a cloud of smoke? Daniel wondered.

"Now Harry's grandmother, Maisie, she lived to be one hundred and two and she always said …" continued Duncan.

"Duncan, look up at the sky. Do you think that is a cloud of smoke over there?" Daniel said, interrupting Duncan's description of Maisie, the centenarian.

"What? Did you say you saw smoke, Danny?" asked Duncan.

"Yes, look up. I am certain of it now. It looks like it is over there, in the west, near the old Turkish part of the city."

Both of them stood up to get a better idea of what they were looking at.

"Yes Danny, you're right, it does look like smoke. It's probably coming from one of those kitchen fires that happen all the time over there in the old town. I am sure they'll put it out soon."

Daniel was not convinced. If anything, it appeared as though the cloud was getting darker and slowly moving in their direction. Daniel inhaled deeply and thought he could detect a faint smell of smoke.

"Duncan, I have a feeling this fire may be a bit bigger than you realize. Breathe in deeply, you can smell it." Duncan did as Daniel advised.

"Danny, I think you're right. Maybe this fire has gotten a little out of hand. Oh, those poor people down there. I do hope no one gets hurt."

In an instant, Daniel thought of something. The Allatini Orphanage was near the area where the smoke seemed to be coming from. "Duncan," said Daniel, sounding worried, "the fire may be near the orphanage, near Gavriel. I must go and make sure that he is safe."

"Danny, I don't think that's wise. You could end up breathing in a lot of smoke and that could be very dangerous, dangerous for your lungs, that is. No, I wouldn't advise it. I am sure the little newspaper boy is fine. Sounds like that orphanage director is a very responsible person. I am certain he is keeping the boys out of harm's way."

"No, Duncan, I must go," said Daniel shaking his head vigorously. "I need to see for myself that Gavriel is safe. I will be back as soon as I can," and with that, Daniel began to walk away quickly.

"Danny, wait, wait. I don't want you to go alone. I'll come with you," Duncan called after him, and he soon caught up with his friend.

The two soldiers quickly headed west in the direction of the fire.

The large grey cloud of smoke grew increasingly menacing as Daniel and Duncan approached the Allatini Orphanage. The smell of smoke was now unmistakable. Many people were standing outside on the street talking excitedly to one another. It seemed to Daniel that they were trying to decide what to do, as though they had just now begun to realize that a fire was raging somewhere in the city and that there was a possibility that it might reach them.

Daniel and Duncan went up the front path to the orphanage. Finding the front door to the building wide open, they quickly went inside and looked around the empty building. They ran down the main corridor, looking for someone, anyone, who might tell them where the boys were. Finally, they came to the large main dining room near the back of the building. From the doorway, they could see a middle-aged man wearing a fez standing at the head of two rows of boys. Daniel understood immediately that this must be Mr. Capon.

It was clear that Mr. Capon was trying his best to remain calm and to keep his voice steady. The boys looked scared, confused and young, very young. Neither Daniel nor Duncan could understand what the director was saying because he was speaking in Ladino, but it soon became clear that he was checking to make sure that all of the boys were there.

"Now, listen carefully," Mr. Capon instructed. "For safety reasons, all of us are soon going to be heading west. Before we leave, I must make certain that all of you are here. Answer 'yes' when your name is called. Quickly now."

"Sabatino."

"Yes."

"Mercado."

"Yes."

"Rachamim."

"Yes."

"Yona."

"Yes."

Suddenly, Daniel remembered that this was the name of the boy Gavriel had mentioned as being his friend.

"That's Yona, Gavriel's friend," he whispered to Duncan.

As the director continued to call the names, Daniel quickly scanned the two rows of boys. He did not see Gavriel. Where was he?

"Gavriel," called Mr. Capon. No one answered. "Gavriel," he called again, louder this time. There was no answer. The director looked around the room and his eyes suddenly met Daniel's.

Startled, Mr. Capon asked, in heavily accented English, "Who are you?"

Daniel replied quickly, "I am Daniel Sheinfeld, Private, 60th 2nd/2nd London Division. I am a friend of Gavriel Florentin's. I came to make sure that he was safe. Where is he?"

Mr. Capon could not answer. He did not know. He said, his voice rising, "Boys, where is Gavriel? Who has seen him?" The boys exchanged puzzled looks and remained silent; no one had seen Gavriel since lunchtime.

"Boys!" Mr. Capon said, his voice even more anxious. "Who was the last person to see Gavriel? Tell me, tell me right now!" From the very back of the line, a timid voice said, "It may have been me, Mr. Capon."

"Sebi, why didn't you speak up earlier?" Mr. Capon shouted.

"Well, I wasn't sure, I mean, that is, I saw him leaving the orphanage after lunch," Sebi said, his voice wavering. Daniel did not understand what had just been said, but he had a sense that this boy, this Sebi, knew something about Gavriel's whereabouts.

Yona called out to Sebi from his place in line. "Did Gavriel seem upset when he left? Was something bothering him?" Sebi replied so quietly that it was almost impossible to hear him. "Yes, I guess so. I guess he was a little upset."

"Boys, boys!" Mr. Capon interrupted, his voice getting even louder. "This is not the time for a conversation. We must leave. It is not safe for us to remain here any longer. For the last time, does anybody have any idea where Gavriel might be?" Mr. Capon demanded.

Yona looked up at Mr. Capon and said sadly, "Yes, sir, I think I may know where he is."

"Where is he? Where is he?" Mr. Capon shouted at Yona.

"I think he may be at the *Italia Yashan* synagogue," Yona replied.

"Where? At the synagogue? Why would he have gone to the *Italia Yashan* in the middle of the afternoon?" Mr. Capon shouted.

Yona answered hesitantly. "He showed me once, there is a little room there, upstairs, in the women's section. He used to play there as a child. He told me that sometimes he would go there when he was feeling lonely, when he missed his mother, and he would just sit there for a while."

Mr. Capon turned to Daniel and briefly translated what Yona had just told him. Without stopping to think, Daniel immediately instructed him, "Mr. Capon, take the rest of the boys out of the neighborhood. Private McPhee and I will go to the synagogue. We will find Gavriel and take him to safety."

"Yes, yes, we will go at once," concurred Duncan, who had not understood most of what had just transpired but knew that his help was needed.

"Fine. Go to the synagogue. Find the boy and take him somewhere safe. Later, after this fire has been put out, I will manage to find him." Without saying anything further, Mr. Capon turned to the children.

"Boys, let's go." The boys quickly followed Mr. Capon out of the room and down the hall to the courtyard. As the director opened the back door, they were met by a thick haze of smoke.

**D**aniel and Duncan were shocked by the chaotic scene that greeted them as they approached the area near the *Italia Yashan* synagogue.

The narrow interconnected streets and alleys of the city were packed with crowds of terrified people, all of whom were desperately trying to flee the fire and head to the safety of the waterfront.

People of all ages were shouting, crying and screaming in a multitude of languages – Turkish, Greek, Ladino, English and French. Men, women and children alike were trying to hold on to their meager possessions – mirrors, pots, sewing machines, blankets, dishes and linens. Greek boy scouts and troops of multinational soldiers were desperately trying to impose a semblance of order amidst the chaos.

By now, it was clear to all of the inhabitants of Salonika that the fire was raging out of control. Fueled in part by the intense north wind blowing off of the Vardar River, the fire had begun in the Turkish quarter and had spread toward the center of the city, rapidly devouring building after building with its ferocious appetite.

The archaic fire engines belonging to the city were completely ineffectual; at best, they spat out thin streams of water. Two British fire engines and two large crews of British firefighters tried desperately to contain the fire, but they had difficulty maneuvering their trucks in and out of the narrow streets.

A number of British and French soldiers were trying to guide the panic-stricken citizens to the direction of the waterfront, reassuring them that they would find shelter on the various battleships. Other soldiers were hastily loading people onto army issue trucks and vans, telling them that they would be ferried to a safer part of the city, further to the east.

The dense columns of thick grey smoke and the general confusion of the area made it difficult for Daniel and Duncan to find the *Italia Yashan* synagogue. As it finally came into view, the full horror of the scene became apparent – the synagogue was on fire!

"Look, look, the *Italia Yashan* is on fire," screamed Daniel.

Daniel raced over to the synagogue, with Duncan following behind him as quickly as his injured leg would allow. A number of British soldiers were standing near the synagogue, trying valiantly to direct people out of harm's way.

"I must go inside!" Daniel yelled at one of the soldiers.

"Get inside? Are you insane? The whole building is going to go up in flames in a matter of minutes!"

"There is a young boy inside! I must go inside!" Daniel repeated.

The soldier turned to Duncan and said, "Is your friend mad? He wants to run into this building."

Duncan turned to Daniel and entreated, "Danny, Danny, you can't go inside. The building is on fire. You don't even know that Gavriel is in there!" Duncan pleaded, "Please, Danny, it's dangerous, don't go, don't go into the fire. We're going home this week. Please, Danny …"

Ignoring Duncan's pleas, Daniel ran toward the front entrance of the building. As soon as he got inside, he was immediately overcome by a thick wall of smoke and he started to cough. He quickly took his handkerchief from his pocket and held it over his mouth and nose, tying it to the back of his head. He had never been inside the synagogue before and was not sure where the stairs were.

Completed blinded by smoke and coughing deeply, Daniel held out his hands in front of him until he managed to find the stairs. Climbing three at a time, he reached the ladies' section quickly.

Daniel did not know where the flames were, but he could tell from the intense heat here, on the upper level, that the fire would soon engulf the ladies' section.

He remembered Mr. Capon telling him that Yona had said that the little room was in the right-hand corner of the room. Daniel stumbled among the pews until he found his way to the far wall. Running his hands against the flat surface, he searched for a doorknob, frantically trying to find the door that opened to the little room.

After what seemed like an eternity, Daniel's right hand brushed against something very hot – a metal doorknob. Trying to ignore the pain, he twisted the knob and managed to open the small door. In order to fit his tall frame inside the tiny room, Daniel dropped to his knees. He entered the room, and almost immediately, he bumped up against a small body lying on the floor.

Still on his knees, he grabbed hold of the motionless figure by the shoulders and dragged him out of the room. Then Daniel stood up, scooped the boy into his arms and headed in the direction of a dim light that he hoped was coming from a nearby window.

By the time Daniel had reached the window, he was coughing uncontrollably. He was drenched in sweat and his uniform was completely covered in soot. His eyes were watering so much that he could barely see, and his right hand throbbed painfully.

Cradling Gavriel's body in his left arm, Daniel leaned back, and with one single, determined motion, he kicked open the window with his right foot. The sound of shattered glass pierced the darkness.

From outside, Daniel could hear the unmistakable voice of his friend Duncan screaming, "Stand back! Stand back! I've got him, I've got him!"

In order to achieve the necessary momentum, Daniel ran back a few steps. Then, holding his long arms tightly around the small, motionless body, he squeezed his eyes shut and ran forward, throwing himself out of the window.

Daniel landed safely in the Scotsman's enormous embrace.

**D**aniel was resting in bed, his head lying on top of two army issue pillows. As soon as he saw Duncan enter the room, Daniel looked up and began to bombard him with questions. "What were you able to find out? How is he? Where did they take him?"

Daniel and Gavriel had been separated right after Daniel had jumped out of the window. Daniel had been sent back to the hospital where he had been for the past four months, but no one seemed to know where Gavriel had been taken.

Daniel's right hand was badly burned and he had numerous cuts on his right leg where he had kicked open the window. His lungs, already damaged by his bout of pneumonia, had been compromised even further. He was very weak, but the hospital staff felt that, all things considered, he was in remarkably good shape.

Duncan took a seat on the vacant bed beside Daniel. "Danny, the little newspaper boy is in one of the British military hospital ships moored at the harbor. Even though an enormous part of the city has been burned to the ground, luckily, there was little damage to the port. The British and the French soldiers took a lot of local people there and somehow, Gavriel ended up on a British hospital ship."

"How is he?" Daniel asked anxiously.

"Well, I spoke to one of the nurses and she said that he is conscious, but that he is suffering the effects of severe smoke inhalation – shortness of breath, headache and hoarseness when he talks. He is also coughing a lot," Duncan answered.

"You didn't see him yourself?" Daniel asked, sounding disappointed. "No, Danny, I am sorry. I asked, but the nurse said that he is not allowed visitors right now. They are keeping a close eye on him."

Daniel thought about all of this for a minute. "Duncan, what about the other boys in the orphanage, and Mr. Capon? Have you heard anything about them?"

"Well, Danny, in a matter of speaking, I did. When I asked the nurse if I could see the little newspaper boy, she told me that another man, accompanied by a group of children, had been around earlier in the morning also asking to see him. I think this must have been Mr. Capon."

"Yes, Duncan, I am sure that you're right. What I need to do now, of course, is to speak to Mr. Capon. The day before the fire, I told Gavriel that I would speak to Mr. Capon on his behalf and find out why he still had not made arrangements for him to be sent to his aunt and uncle in Leeds."

"Danny, give yourself a few days' rest. You have to regain

your strength. You have been through quite an ordeal and ..." Duncan's face broke into a wide smile, "You are quite famous."

"Famous? What do you mean, 'famous'?" asked Daniel, sounding uneasy.

"Well, let's just say that there is an article about you today in *The Daily Star*," Duncan replied.

Duncan now presented Daniel with a newspaper that had been tucked under his arm. "Second page, my friend. Read it and see for yourself."

Daniel read the article and was quite amazed. "Duncan, really, this is all quite embarrassing. I don't want people to think of me as a hero," he said.

"I am sorry, Danny, it's a bit too late for that!" Duncan said, beaming proudly at his friend.

"Duncan, what about you? You haven't said a word about your plans. When is the ship set to sail?"

Duncan replied with evident excitement. "Six p.m. sharp, this evening. And believe me, I won't be late. No, sir! Now listen, Danny, this is what I want to do. On my way home, I want to stop off briefly in London. I want to see your parents, tell them about what has happened to you and let them know that you will be coming home soon. What do you think?"

Daniel was overwhelmed by Duncan's kindheartedness. He was not sure what to say.

"Danny, what's wrong? Don't you like this idea?" asked Duncan.

"Duncan, of course I like the idea. My parents and my sisters would love to meet you, and they would be thrilled to learn that I am coming home soon. But you have already done so much for me. Do you really want to delay your homecoming?"

"Oh, Danny, the McPhees can wait another day to see me. Don't worry about that!" Duncan reassured him.

Duncan eventually persuaded Daniel that it would be no trouble at all to go and visit Daniel's family. The two of them then exchanged addresses and phone numbers.

It was now time for Duncan to leave. As he got up, he looked directly at Daniel. "Daniel, I cannot tell you how proud I am of you! Have a good rest, and come home soon. As we say in Scotland, 'Aye, to be sure, the angels of the good Lord himself will be weeping' at the sight of the graceful footwork of Private Sheinfeld."

Daniel, of course, had no idea what Duncan had said to him, but he could tell that the words were heartfelt, and he appreciated the sentiment.

With every passing day, Daniel began to feel stronger. He was increasingly anxious to see Gavriel, but he was not sure where Gavriel was. Although Duncan had told him that Gavriel was in a British hospital ship at the port, Daniel had not thought to ask which ship he was on, and now Duncan was on his way home.

He assumed that Mr. Capon would know where Gavriel had been sent, but the director was even more difficult to locate than Gavriel.

In the wake of the fire, thousands upon thousands of people had been evacuated from their homes. They were now scattered in relief camps in and around Salonika, and some of them had already left the city completely.

The British army had set up three large tent settlements that accommodated over 7,000 people, and the French army had established two such settlements, which housed another 2,000 people. Another 5,000 people had been taken to Athens and other Greek cities nearby. It might take Daniel weeks to locate Mr. Capon.

He realized that the only option was for him to walk down to the port himself and begin searching in each of the hospital ships. He knew that this would have to wait a few more days until he had regained a bit more of his strength.

*London*
*September 5, 1917*

Duncan looked at his watch. It was now almost five p.m., and his train to Inverary was scheduled to depart at seven. *I have more than enough time to meet Danny's parents*, Duncan said to himself as he approached Sheinfeld's Bakery.

He had arrived at the port in Southampton earlier in the day and had immediately boarded a train that brought him to Victoria Station in London. It had been a long, tiring journey and his bad leg was beginning to ache, but he kept his spirits up by imagining how happy Daniel's parents would be to have news of their son.

From the window, Duncan could see two young women standing behind the counter. He knew immediately that they were Daniel's sisters – the family resemblance was extraordinary.

He pushed the door open and went inside. As he looked at the two young women, he tried very hard to remember their names. Daniel had showed him a family photo once and had told him that Yetta was the oldest and that the second one was called Hennie, or was it the other

CHAPTER THIRTY-FIVE

way around? And the little one, the one that wrote Daniel all those letters, what was her name? Daniel said it was the Hebrew equivalent of Deborah. Or was it maybe Dora? No, no, it was De–vo–ra.

As Duncan walked over to the counter, one of the sisters looked up at him. It was obvious from her startled expression that large, heavyset Argyll and Sutherland Highlanders dressed in full uniform rarely, if ever, patronized Sheinfeld's Bakery.

"May I help you, sir?" she politely inquired. Duncan paused for a moment, debating with himself if he should attempt to guess which sister she was. *Oh, why not?* he decided.

"Hello, Miss … Miss Hennie, is it?

The young woman flushed and said, "Yes, well, actually my first name is Henia. Do I know you, sir?"

"No, Miss Henia, but I have heard a lot about you, and your sisters and your parents, too. I am a good friend of your brother's," Duncan replied with a broad smile.

"A friend of Daniel's!" she exclaimed. Turning to her sister she said, "Yetta, this soldier is a friend of Daniel's!" The two sisters looked at Duncan and said, almost in unison, "How is he?"

"Your brother is fine. I just saw him a few days ago and he is doing well. I would like to talk to your parents, if they are available," Duncan said. "Why, certainly, certainly, Mr. … Mr. …," said Henia.

"Please, call me Duncan," he replied.

Henia quickly headed to the back of the bakery and

bounded up the stairs to find her parents. She threw open the front door of their flat. "Mama, Papa, hurry! Come quickly! There is a soldier downstairs, a friend of Daniel's. He just walked into the shop a few minutes ago and introduced himself, and he wants to meet you!"

"A friend of Daniel's, here, from the army, right now, downstairs?!" her father exclaimed excitedly. "Esthereva, Devora, come, come, we must meet him!"

The four of them hurried down the stairs and quickly went into the bakery. There stood Duncan, introducing himself to a man who had just bought a quarter loaf of *brahnbroit*.

Mottel approached him, stuck out his hand and said, "Hello, I am Mottel Sheinfeld and this is my wife, Esthereva." Duncan shook Mottel's hand, nodding in Esthereva's direction.

"My name is Duncan McPhee, and I am very pleased to meet you." Then, spotting Devora standing beside her mother, he said, "And you, young lass, must be Devora."

"Yes, yes, I am Devora Sheinfeld. How did you know my name?" she asked.

"Well, you see, I am good friends with your brother Danny, I mean, your brother Daniel. We spent a lot of time together in Salonika, and he told me all about his family. And all about you, in particular." Devora beamed at Duncan.

"Do you have news about my son?" asked Mottel, anxious to hear about Daniel. "Yes, Mr. Sheinfeld, I certainly do. I have wonderful news for you. Daniel is scheduled to come home within the month!" Duncan announced.

"Within the month? *Baruch Hashem!* A month! Esthereva, did you hear that? This is wonderful news, wonderful," Mottel exclaimed.

And then, suddenly, a look of concern appeared on Mottel's face. "Mr. McPhee," he began hesitantly.

"No, no, call me Duncan," Duncan interjected.

"Fine, Duncan. Has my son been injured? Is that why he is being sent home?" Mottel asked, sounding worried.

From inside the shirt pocket of his uniform, Duncan retrieved a newspaper article. He thrust it into Mottel's hands and said, "Your son is fine. Read this."

"Papa, Papa, read it out loud so all of us can hear," pleaded Devora. Mottel shot a questioning glance at Duncan.

"Yes, yes, by all means. I am sure your entire family would enjoy hearing this."

Mottel cleared his throat and began to read:

## BRITISH PRIVATE SAVES ORPHAN BOY

In the midst of the tremendous destruction and devastation wreaked on our fair city yesterday, one story has emerged that has touched the hearts of people all over Salonika. Private Daniel Sheinfeld, 19, of the 60th 2nd/2nd London Division rushed into a burning synagogue late yesterday afternoon and saved the life of a young Saloniki boy. Eyewitnesses said that Private Sheinfeld, against the advice of other

British soldiers on the scene, insisted on running into the building, believing, correctly, that a young boy was trapped inside. Private Sheinfeld found the boy lying unconscious on the upper storey and, in a true act of heroism, shattered a window with his right foot and jumped out, holding the boy in his arms. Private Sheinfeld and the boy were caught by a quick-acting bystander. Private Sheinfeld is now recuperating from minor injuries he sustained from the ordeal. The young boy, who has been identified as Gavriel Florentin, is suffering from the effects of smoke inhalation. Both are currently in local hospitals and are expected to recover fully. Gruna Kroit, who identified herself as a close personal friend of Private Sheinfeld's, spoke to this reporter and said, "I always knew that Daniel was special. I am proud to say that this hero is my very dear friend."

"Esthereva, did you hear all of this?" Mottel shouted. "Did you hear what our son did? Girls, girls, your brother, he is a hero! He saved a life! He saved a little boy's life! Oh, Mr. McPhee, I mean, Duncan, thank you so much for visiting us and for bringing us this article." Mottel went over to shake the soldier's hand a second time, and as he did so, he dropped the newspaper article on the floor.

"Papa, you dropped the newspaper article," said Devora as she bent down to pick it up.

As Mottel, Esthereva, Henia and Yetta were talking

animatedly to Duncan, Devora looked at the newspaper article. She noticed that there was a picture of a young boy at the bottom. The boy looked familiar to her – thick dark hair, round expressive eyes – as if she had somehow seen his face before. But how could this be? He was a young Saloniki boy, and she had never been outside of the East End of London.

All of a sudden Devora thought of something. Taking the newspaper article with her, she hurried to the back of the bakery. She grabbed an old wooden box that was lying nearby and climbed on top of it so she would be tall enough to see the wall of messages. Yes, there it was, right in the middle. There was that photograph – the one that the man with the strange accent had left here all those months ago. Studying the photo on the wall and the picture in the paper, she realized it was the same boy.

She carefully removed the photo from the wall – for her mother had cautioned her to never touch the photo – and hurried back to her family. "Mama, Papa, it is the same boy," she declared.

"What? What are you talking about?" asked her mother.

"The boy in the newspaper, the boy Daniel saved, it is the same boy as the one in the photo on our wall. I am sure of it. Look." Devora put both pictures down on the counter, side by side.

Yetta was the first one to take a look. "Oh, my goodness, Devora is right! It *is* the same boy," she shouted.

"Girls, please calm yourselves. Let me take a closer look,"

said their mother. She held up both pictures close to her face and examined them intently.

Mottel asked Duncan, "Would you by any chance know anything about this boy, this, this, Gavriel?"

"Of course. He is a Jewish child, around eleven or twelve years old or so. He was very helpful to Daniel. Showed him around, took him to the shops, things like that."

"A Jewish boy?" Mottel repeated, as if he couldn't quite understand what Duncan had just told him.

"Yes, yes, he is a Jewish boy. He wears the sacred fringes and a skullcap, and he eats the same special food, and he goes to the synagogue," Duncan elaborated.

"I see," said Mottel, trying to think all of this through. "Did he ever mention having family here, in England, by any chance?"

"Yes, in fact, he did mention that he had an aunt and uncle, in Leeds," replied Duncan.

"Mottel, I have looked at the pictures very carefully and I think Devora is right – it is the same boy," said Esthereva.

Esthereva hurried over to a small wooden drawer behind the bakery counter and began to rummage through the odd bits of string, pencils and papers that she kept there.

In a minute, she pulled out a small piece of paper and said excitedly, "Here it is, here it is! This is the information the man gave me that afternoon, all those months ago: Gedalia and Perla Perahia, 11, Earlscourt Lane, Leeds. Telephone 555-5482."

"We must call these people at once! At once!" Mottel exclaimed.

Duncan was so engrossed in the unfolding drama that he had completely forgotten to keep his eye on the time. He now looked at his watch. It was much later than he realized. No doubt he would miss the 7 p.m. train to Inverary. Duncan didn't really mind. He felt compelled to stay and find out if these people named Perahia were indeed the little newspaper boy's aunt and uncle.

The family went to the back of the shop where the telephone was located. With trembling hands, Mottel picked up the receiver and asked the operator to connect him. It rang a few times and then a man picked up.

"Hello, sir, may I please speak with Mr. Gedalia Perahia?"

"Speaking," answered a male voice.

"Sir, this is Mottel Sheinfeld calling, from Sheinfeld's Bakery in London," said Mottel.

"Yes?" queried the man. "May I help you?"

"Mr. Perahia, we have a soldier in our bakery at the moment, a soldier returning home from Salonika, who brought us news of a young boy ...."

"Yes, please continue, Mr. Sheinfeld," said the male voice, his voice rising with increased interest.

"The boy lives in Salonika and he is well. He is fine. His name is Gavriel Florentin."

"Gavriel! Gavriel! *Gracias al Dio! Santo Bendicho! Perla, vene aqui, vene aqui presto* (Thank *Hashem*! Bless *Hashem*! Perla, come here, come here quickly)!" Mottel could hear Mr. Perahia calling to someone in the background.

"Mr. Perahia, excuse me, Mr. Perahia, I am sorry, but am I to understand that this is the boy whom you were looking for?" Mottel asked hopefully.

"Oh, yes, yes, Mr. Sheinfeld," Mr. Perahia answered, his voice breaking. "The boy is our nephew! He is the son of my wife's late sister, her sister Allegra. Please, please tell me everything."

Mottel, with the enthusiastic assistance of Duncan, talked to Gedalia Perahia for some time, telling him all that he knew. Esthereva, Henia and Yetta sat nearby and listened with interest to the whole story.

Devora listened, too, but she was distracted by one delightful thought – her and Daniel's mission had been a success. All those months ago, right before he had been shipped out, Daniel had told her that the two of them had something important to do, that they had a mission. In every letter that she had sent him, she had asked her brother if he had found their mission yet. And, indeed, this afternoon, here in the bakery, it was finally revealed to her, just as Daniel had said that it would be.

It was obvious to Devora. Daniel had saved Gavriel's life by getting him out of that burning building and she, Devora, had recognized him in the local newspaper. In doing so, both of them had brought Gavriel back to his family.

Their mission completed, Devora knew that it was now time for Daniel to come home.

# CHAPTER THIRTY-SIX

**A** flurry of arrangements followed Mottel Sheinfeld's phone call to Gedalia Perahia. Within two weeks, plans had been finalized for Gavriel to travel to England with Daniel aboard a British military ship.

Perla was overjoyed that she was finally going to be reunited with her sister's child. She and her husband had spent endless months trying to find Gavriel. They had written letters, sent numerous telegrams and tried to contact whomever they thought might be able to help them in Salonika, but the only thing they had been able to ascertain was that the Benvenistes had moved.

One afternoon, as Perla was busy organizing the room in her house that was soon to become Gavriel's bedroom, she was overwhelmed by a feeling of apprehension. How was her young nephew going to be able to adjust to life in Leeds?

She suddenly realized that she and her husband were sending a twelve year old boy across the sea and bringing him to a completely foreign country. By doing so, they were removing him from everything he had always known. The boy had already been through so much – too much. How would he cope?

Perla worried about this for many days, and she found herself constantly wondering what her late sister Allegra would have wanted her to do. What would be best for Gavriel?

After talking about this with her husband, and then speaking with Mr. Capon over the phone, Perla believed that she had a solution.

One afternoon, with the intense summer sun beating down upon them, Mr. Capon and the boys from the orphanage stood at the port. The British military ship was set to leave shortly, and all of them had come to say good-bye to Gavriel, and to another boy, as well.

The Perahias had decided to adopt Yona. They hoped that having Yona by his side would help ease Gavriel's transition to his new life in England, and they were happy to provide a home for the orphan whom Mr. Capon had described as a sweet and gentle boy, and who had been a loyal and devoted friend to Gavriel.

As Mr. Capon spoke to Daniel about the ship's route, each boy took turns saying good-bye to Yona and Gavriel. All of them were very happy for the boys, but they knew that they would miss both of them.

Mr. Capon warmly embraced Gavriel and Yona. He

advised them not to be worried about the voyage because it was well known that *"Quien gasta en lo seco, come en la mar* (He who does well on land will do well at sea)."

After everyone had said good-bye, there remained only one person who had not said anything to Gavriel, Yona and Daniel, and that was Sebi.

Since arriving at the port, Sebi had stood at a considerable distance from the rest of the group with a troubled, anxious look on his face. He desperately wanted to say something to Gavriel, but he just didn't know how. But now, as he saw Gavriel and Yona begin to follow Daniel up the gangplank, he knew that he must act immediately or lose the opportunity.

Taking a deep breath, for he was about to do something that he had never done before, he came closer to the gangplank and called after the boys, "Wait, wait, there is something that I need to tell you." Gavriel and Yona turned their heads back toward the port and saw to their surprise that it was Sebi who had called after them. They stopped walking.

Sebi came over to the side of the gangplank and said quietly, "I am truly sorry, Gavriel, for the way that I treated you. I hope that you will forgive me."

Gavriel looked at Sebi and without a moment's hesitation said, "Of course, Sebi, I forgive you." Sebi, exhaling deeply, looked intently at Gavriel for a second and then walked away. He now went to stand with the rest of the group.

Noticing that Gavriel and Yona had paused for a moment,

Daniel called to them, "Come along, boys. We don't want the ship to leave without us," as he continued walking up the gangplank.

Yona and Gavriel hurried after Daniel. They turned back one last time to smile and wave good-bye. Everyone smiled and waved back – everyone, including Sebi.

**G**avriel and Yona were initially quite seasick, as neither of them had ever been
to sea and they were not used to the constant,
rocking motion of the ship. However, by the
time they reached Athens two days later, they
were feeling considerably more comfortable
on board.

When the ship docked, the passengers were
told that they had three hours to walk around
the city. As they were about to disembark,
Daniel told both boys that if they hurried,
they might have time to see the *Etz Hayyim*
Synagogue, and maybe even have a chance to
meet Pini Conforti, the hospitable Greek *gabbai* that Daniel had told them all about.

As soon as Daniel and the boys started to
walk away from the port, a man in a small
brown truck pulled up directly in front of them.
He called from the open window, in Greek,
"*Epi telous, epi telous, eisai edo epi telous* (At last,
at last, you're here! You're here at last)!"

Gavriel quickly translated what the man had
said. The man stopped the truck and jumped
out. He ran over to Daniel and exclaimed,

*"Danil! Se perimena!* (Daniel! I've been waiting for you!)" Daniel was sure the man had mistaken him for someone else, until he took a closer look. And then, Daniel's face broke into a wide smile of recognition, for it was the Greek *gabbai* himself – Pini! Pini Conforti!

The two men shook hands warmly and then, with Gavriel translating, Pini told Daniel what he was doing at the port.

Pini had read about Daniel's act of heroism in one of the local papers, and he knew from the paper that Daniel had been injured. He was certain that Daniel would be invalided home, and he had correctly assumed that any British military ship bound for England would make a stop in Athens.

For the past few weeks, whenever Pini heard that a British military ship was arriving in the city, he would go down to the port and look at the passengers to see if Daniel was among them. Pini guessed that he came down to the port two to three times a week.

Daniel was amazed that Pini had gone to all this trouble just to see him. But before Daniel had a chance to say anything, Pini went back into his truck and returned in a matter of seconds, proudly holding a small blue velvet bag.

Daniel recognized the bag immediately – it was his *tefillin* bag! He couldn't believe it, after all this time! The *tefillin* his father had bought him, just before his *bar mitzvah*; he never thought he would see it again! Pini handed the *tefillin* to Daniel, who held it gratefully in his hands.

Pini told Daniel that he had found the *tefillin* at the synagogue the morning after Daniel had departed for Salonika.

Although he had tried to contact the British military author-
ities in the city, he had had no success. He had safeguarded
the *tefillin* at his house, hoping that eventually, when the war
was over and Daniel was sent back to England, he would
stop in Athens and Pini would be able to return it to him.

Pini invited Daniel and the boys to his house for lunch.
Daniel shook his head and said to Gavriel, "Tell Pini that we
don't want to put his wife to any trouble."

Gavriel relayed the message and Pini replied with a dis-
missive wave of his hand, saying, "Please, don't worry. My
wife Alvina has enough food to feed at least twenty people!"

Daniel and the boys spent an enjoyable three hours with
Pini, and late in the afternoon, he drove them back to the
port. Daniel gave Pini his address in England and told Pini
that he should come and visit. Pini smiled at Daniel and said,
"You never know. I may surprise you one day."

Right before they were about to embark, Daniel told
Gavriel to ask Pini a question that had been on his mind the
entire afternoon. What had motivated Pini to help Daniel in
such a generous, kindhearted way?

Pini Conforti smiled. With Gavriel translating, he
answered, "My family, the Confortis, have a long and well-
established practice of helping Jewish travelers. This tradi-
tion goes back to my great-grandfather, Mordu Conforti,
who once helped a large group of Jews who found themselves
stranded in Bulgaria."

Daniel, Gavriel and Yona would have loved to hear the
story, but they knew that time did not allow for it. Daniel

led the two boys back onto the ship and tucked his *tefillin* from home safely under his arm. As he did so, it occurred to Daniel that he now had the perfect gift to give Gavriel when he would become bar mitzvahed – the very *tefillin* Gavriel had helped Daniel buy in Salonika!

# CHAPTER THIRTY-EIGHT

*Victoria Station, London*
*September 1917*

The route that Daniel, Gavriel and Yona took to England was much the same as the one Daniel had initially taken to Salonika, but in reverse. From Athens they sailed to the French port city of Marseilles, and from there they boarded a train to Le Havre, in northern France. There, they crossed the English Channel and arrived at Southampton.

It was a long, tiring trip, and by the time the three of them arrived at the station in London, they were exhausted, but elated.

As they left the train, Daniel said to Gavriel and Yona, "If I am correct, I think we need to leave the station from the upper level. Stay together. It is very crowded here."

The three of them began to negotiate their way among the mass of people exiting the train. All of a sudden, Daniel heard the sound of a curt, authoritarian voice. He recognized it immediately.

"Sheinfeld," said an older, tired-looking soldier as he approached Daniel.

Daniel responded, "Yes, Sergeant."

"Sheinfeld, come here."

"Yes, Sergeant," Daniel replied again.

Gavriel and Yona stared at this curmudgeon, who spoke in such a clipped, brusque manner that it was hard to understand what he was saying. Could this be Sergeant Pape, the soldier Daniel had told them about? The soldier who had been in charge of Daniel and his group of friends during their basic training at the Tower of London?

"Sheinfeld, you are certainly aware that in a few days' time you will be discharged from the army, due to the injuries you sustained in Salonika."

"Yes, Sergeant," replied Daniel, wondering why he was telling him something that he already knew.

"I most probably will not see you again. I wanted to tell you how proud I am of your actions in Salonika. You displayed tremendous bravery and you brought honor to the 60th 2nd/2nd London Division, even though your actions were not conducted in the line of duty. You've done well, lad."

"Thank you," replied Daniel.

Sergeant Pape paused for a split second, and Daniel thought that he could detect just the hint of a smile on his face. Sergeant Pape said, "That is all, Sheinfeld. Carry on." Then he abruptly turned and walked away from the platform.

Although Gavriel and Yona had not understood much of what had been said, they could tell from the look on Daniel's face that he was very touched by the older soldier's words.

As Daniel continued to lead the boys along the platform and up the stairs, he mused to himself how amazing it was that the events of the past ten months had been initiated by Sergeant Pape.

Pape had noticed Daniel's skills during basic training and had recommended him for the signaler's course. This had resulted in Daniel being sent to Salonika, instead of to the Western Front.

Little had Daniel known that it would be there, in Salonika, that he would achieve something so important.

At the time, being separated from his group of friends and being sent to Salonika had been deeply upsetting to Daniel. But now, in retrospect, Daniel realized that all of this had been part of something larger, something that he could not see at the time. It was just as Gavriel had told him that day at the White Tower. What we see in front of us at any given time is not the way things really are ….

Daniel led the boys upstairs. As they came close to the exit, they began to hear a lot of noise. A large number of people seemed to be calling and shouting all at once. "Daniel! Daniel! Welcome home!"

"The hero is here!"

"Private Sheinfeld, how are you?"

"Look, I see him, I see him."

Daniel, Gavriel and Yona walked in the direction of the commotion. They were soon overwhelmed by a crowd of thirty or so people, standing all together. Among them were young children, older women and British soldiers. At the very front of the group stood Daniel's parents and sisters.

Daniel's mother immediately broke free of the crowd and

ran over to embrace her son. She threw her arms around his neck.

"Oh, my son, my son! *Hashem* has answered my prayers! *Hashem* has returned you to me."

The rest of the family hurried over to Daniel and gave him an enormous hug. Daniel noticed that his father's eyes were full of tears, and Daniel realized that he, too, was crying.

As Daniel brushed away his tears, he felt Devora grab his hand. He smiled down at her.

"Daniel, we did it! We did it! We accomplished our mission. You saved Gavriel, and I found him."

Daniel bent down so he would be at eye level with Devora. "Yes," he said in a mock serious tone, "our mission is now complete. Good work, Devora. I knew we could do it." The brother and sister hugged each other tightly.

In the meantime, a tall distinguished-looking couple tentatively approached the two Saloniki boys. Gavriel recognized them right away, although he hadn't seen them in many years. Yona looked cautiously at Gavriel and Gavriel nodded, as if to confirm their identity. Yes, these people were his aunt and uncle.

Gavriel stepped forward and gave Perla and Gedalia a hesitant hug, which was reciprocated with great affection. Gavriel introduced Yona to his aunt and uncle, and they both greeted the boy with wide smiles. The four of them stood and talked to each other in Ladino for several minutes.

Daniel now began to recognize many of the other people standing in the crowd. His Tante Faiga was there, standing beside another older-looking woman. Oh, my goodness, Daniel said to himself – it was Mrs. Finkel, the widow he had delivered bread to for so many years.

Tante Faiga kissed Daniel on his cheek, while Mrs. Finkel looked on admiringly. "Daniel, Daniel, it is wonderful to see you again. I have missed you terribly," she said.

Two young men came over to Daniel. The taller one seemed to be walking very slowly, holding on to the arm of the shorter, chubby one. For a second, Daniel didn't recognize them, and then he realized that these were his friends, Avrumi and Moishe. He was relieved to notice that although Avrumi was walking slowly, he seemed to have recovered from trench foot. Moishe seemed to have recovered as well, for he looked exactly the same as he always had.

Avrumi and Moishe both embraced Daniel. The three old friends stood and chatted until they were interrupted by a number of soldiers who had known Daniel from basic training at the Tower of London.

Each of them congratulated Daniel. Many of them patted him on the back and said, "Good job, Sheinfeld!" and "You have done us proud!"

One soldier managed to maneuver his way to the front of the group. He thrust out his hand and said loudly, "*Baruch haba*." It was Smythe!

Daniel shook his hand and joked, "Smythe, I am sure that you knew I was coming home even before I did!"

Daniel was greeted by many other well-wishers at the station – customers from the bakery, neighbors and parents of Daniel's friends. Among them were Sruli Goldbloom, Menachem Blau and, most touchingly, Chezki's father, Hershel Katz.

After everyone had had a chance to speak to Daniel, his father announced, "I would like to thank all of you for being here with us today. However, we now must be going home. Daniel and the two young boys have had a long trip, and they need their rest." Everyone agreed with him, and the crowd soon dispersed.

It was time for Gavriel and Daniel to say good-bye to each other. Gavriel walked over to Daniel.

"Daniel, how can I ever thank you? What you did for me was unbelievable, incredible. You saved me."

Daniel looked intently at the boy. For the second time in just a few minutes, he thought about what Gavriel had taught him that day at the White Tower.

Daniel then said something that he was certain Gavriel would not understand until he was much older. His voice heavy with emotion, Daniel said, "No, Gavriel … you saved me."

# Glossary

**A"h** – acronym for *aleha hashalom*, may she rest in peace

**Aleichem shalom** – lit., "upon you be peace"; the traditional response to "Shalom aleichem"

**Aron Kodesh** – the holy ark in the synagogue that houses the Torah scrolls

**Bar mitzvah** – the age of thirteen, when a Jewish boy becomes obligated to observe the Torah's commandments

**Baruch haba** – welcome

**Baruch Hashem** – Thank Hashem

**Bentched** (Yidd.) – said Grace after Meals

**Bilkas** (Yidd.) – bread rolls

**Bima** – platform from which the Torah scroll is read in the synagogue

**Bizochos** (Ladino) – cookies

**Bli neder** – without promising

**Brass** – slang for high-ranking staff officers

**Calavasicas** (Ladino) – squash

**Cantonists** – Jewish boys who were forcibly conscripted into the Russian army in the nineteenth century

**Challah** – special braided bread used for meals on the Sabbath and holidays

**Chas v'shalom** – perish the thought

**Cheder** – Jewish elementary school

**Cortijo** (Ladino) – large, square courtyard

**Cuexcos** (Ladino) – dried apricot pits; children collected them and they were like a form of currency

**Daven** (Yidd.) – pray

**Devora** – bee

**Emunah** – faith

**Fijones** (Ladino) – kidney beans and oil and onion

**Frum** – religiously observant

**Gabbai** – synagogue manager

**Habra** (Ladino) – local primary school

**Hamal** (Ladino) – porter

**Kabbalist** – Jewish mystic

**Kaddish** – prayer that sanctifies Hashem's name, customarily recited by mourners

**Kehilla kedosha** – holy congregation

**Kever** – grave

**Kiddush** – blessing made on Friday night that sanctifies the Sabbath

**Klal Yisrael** – the Jewish people

**Ladino** – also known as Judeo Spanish, or *Djidio*, this language was based on Castilian and mixed with Hebrew and Portuguese words.

**Lecha Dodi** – song composed in the sixteenth century by Rabbi Shlomo Alkabetz of Safed, to welcome in the Sabbath

**Limonadas** (Ladino) – lemonades

**Maariv** – evening prayers

**Magen David** – Star of David

**Melitzah yesharah** – a proper intercessor

**Merengena** (Ladino) – eggplant

**Mincha** – afternoon prayers

**Minyan, minyanim** – quorum(s) of ten adult Jewish males required for public prayer

**Mitzvah** – Torah commandment

**Mussaf** – additional prayer recited on the Sabbath and holidays

**Ner tamid** – the eternal light, a lamp in the synagogue that is always lit

**Pepitas** (Ladino) – roasted and salted pumpkin seeds

**Pinzela** (Ladino) –peas

**Reb** – an honorific title, like "Sir"

**Ribbono shel Olam** – Master of the Universe

**Rubi** (Ladino) – teacher

**Sefer** – Torah book

**Senor Del Mundo** (Ladino) – Hashem

**Shabbat, Shabbos** – the Sabbath

**Shabbat Shalom** – lit., "a Sabbath of peace"; traditional Sabbath greeting in Sephardic communities

**Shacharis** – morning prayers

**Shalom aleichem** – lit., "peace be upon you"; a traditional Jewish greeting

**Shema** – fundamental Jewish prayer that proclaims the unity of Hashem

**Shteibel** (Yidd.) – small synagogue

**Shtetl** (Yidd.) – village

**Shul** (Yidd.) – synagogue

**Siddur** – prayer book

**Sofer** – scribe

**Taking the king's shilling** – slang for enlisting in the British Army. It comes from the fact that, upon enlistment, the new soldier is given one shilling, representing payment for his first day of work.

**Tallis katan** – four-cornered garment with *tzitzis* (fringes) worn by Jewish males

**Tante** (Yidd.) – aunt

**Tefillin** – phylacteries; black leather boxes containing scrolls with certain Torah portions, worn by adult Jewish men during prayer

**Tefillos** – prayers

**Tzedaka** – charity

**Tzeischem l'shalom** – farewell

**Tzitzis** – fringes worn on four-cornered garments by Jewish males

**Whizzbang** – Army slang for shell

**Yarmulke** (Yidd.) – skullcap

**Yeshivot** – Torah schools

# Author's Note

*Into the Fire* is a work of historical fiction and as such, most of the characters and many of the events in this book are the products of the author's imagination. However, much of what is contained in these pages is based on historical fact.

By 1914, there were approximately 300,000 Jews in England. Of the 180,000 who lived in London, almost 100,000 were Russian-born Jews who lived in the city's East End. Thousands of Jews had emigrated from Russia at the end of the nineteenth century, fleeing poverty, conscription and the widespread pogroms that followed the assassination of Tsar Alexander the Second in 1881.

The First World War started on June 28, 1914, sparked by the assassination of Archduke Franz Ferdinand, the heir to the Austro-Hungarian throne, by a young man from Serbia. Austria-Hungary declared war on Serbia, and Russia – bound by a treaty to defend Serbia – subsequently declared war on Austria-Hungary. Britain and France were drawn into the war on the side of Russia, and these three countries formed "The Allied Powers," alternately referred to as "The Entente Powers."

Germany, the Ottoman Empire and Bulgaria joined the war on the side of Austria-Hungary. They were called "The Central Powers" or "The Triple Alliance." Both sides erroneously believed that the war would be over in a matter of weeks. However, the war did not end until November 11, 1918. The military death toll was never firmly established, but some historians have estimated it to be over 20,000,000.

This story begins in July 1916, soon after the beginning of the Battle of the Somme. Begun on July 1, 1916, this battle would prove to be one of the largest of the First World War. On the first day alone, the British suffered over 57,000 casualties.

Fifty thousand Jews in all parts of the British Empire served during the First World War. At the onset of the war, over 10,000 Jews in

England volunteered for active service. Initially, there was no conscription in England. It was introduced in January 1916 by the Military Service Act.

Foreign-born Jews were exempt from conscription, but by July 1916, with Britain increasingly desperate for soldiers, Herbert Samuel (1870-1963), the Home Secretary, announced in the House of Commons that any Russian-born subject who did not enlist in the British army would be repatriated back to Russia. This was implemented by an Order in Council in August 1916. In response, Zionist leader Vladimir "Zev" Jabotinsky (1880-1940) proposed the formation of a separate battalion for Jewish soldiers. This eventually materialized in the form of "The Jewish Legion."

Rabbi S. Lipson served as Rabbi of the Hammersmith and West Kensington Synagogue for over twenty-five years, beginning in 1909. He was a chaplain on the home front during the war. In this capacity, he endeavored to meet the needs of the Jewish soldiers while they were still in England. He arranged for the provision of kosher food, matza and other Passover items, and when possible obtained Sabbath leave for the soldiers.

Rabbi Dr. Joseph Hertz (1872-1946) was appointed Chief Rabbi of the United Kingdom in 1913 and retained this position until his death. His book, *The Book of Jewish Thoughts*, was given to each Jewish soldier in Britain.

Reverend Michael Adler served as the Senior Jewish Chaplain on the Western Front. He visited Jewish soldiers on the front and held weekday and Sabbath services. In the fall of 1916, he conducted Rosh Hashana and Yom Kippur services in the small French village of Ancort, and arranged for Jewish soldiers to be brought there from the front lines. He presided over Jewish burials and tried to secure kosher food. In 1922, he wrote *The British Jewry Book of Honour*, a record of the military service of Jews in the British Empire during the World War I.

Daniel Sheinfeld and his friends were trained at the Tower of London and were assigned to the 60th 2nd 2nd London Division. This division did in fact exist, and their insignia really was the bumblebee. Over three hundred Jews were in this division.

Beginning in June 1916, soldiers from the 60th 2nd 2nd division were sent to France. A number of them remained on the Western Front, but the majority were sent to Salonika. Under the command of Major General Edward Bulfin, the soldiers, numbering several thousand men, completed assembly there on December 25, 1916. They joined the British Expeditionary Force under the command of General George Milne. The Allied Army of the Orient was composed of French, British, Serbian and Russian soldiers, the Commander-in-Chief was French General Sarrail.

The soldiers in Salonika spent much of their time digging roads and putting up barbed wire around the city. For this reason, the British public nicknamed them "The Gardeners of Salonika," and the city was given the epithet "The Birdcage."

The division remained in Salonika until June/July 1917 and was then sent to Egypt to join the Palestine campaign. The division was involved in a number of battles in the area, including the capture and defense of Jerusalem, December 26-30, 1917.

Lester "Mike" Pearson (1897-1972) served in Saloinka as a medic in the Canadian Military Corps, and would later become Canada's fourteenth prime minister (1963-1968).

Salonika came under the control of King George I in 1912, as did the rest of Greece. Greece maintained an official position of neutrality but allowed British, Italian and French troops to disembark and set up army bases throughout the region. On July 2, 1917, Greece declared war on the Central Powers, and for the last year of the war, Greece fought alongside the Allies in Serbia.

At the outbreak of the war, there were approximately 80,000 Jews living in Salonika, out of a total population of 150,000. A small Jewish community had existed there since antiquity. Thousands of Jews fleeing religious persecution in Spain and Portugal settled there in the fifteenth and sixteenth centuries. Rabbi Shlomo HaLevi Alkabetz, the kabbalist and mystical poet, author of the famous *Manos Halevi* on *Megillas Esther* and composer of *Lecha Dodi*, was born here in 1505. The Jewish poet Samule Usque (c. 1530-1596) bestowed upon the city the honorific "*Ir V'em B'Yisrael*" (Metropolis and Mother of Israel).

By the early seventeenth century, Salonika was one of the largest Jewish communities in the world. It was a center of Torah scholarship and home to many well-known rabbis. The Jews here spoke Ladino, also known as Judeo-Spanish or Djidio, a language based on Castilian mixed with Hebrew and Portugese words. The community flourished over the years and established numerous religious schools, synagogues and benevolent societies. Jews worked as artisans, shopkeepers and fishermen, and were such an integral part of the commercial life of the city that most businesses closed early on Friday afternoons.

There were a fair number of wealthy Jewish businessmen in the city, among them the Allatini family, who were mill owners and philanthropists. They gave their name to a variety of social welfare institutions, including an orphanage for Jewish children.

The Great Fire of 1917 began on Saturday, August 18, 1917, at approximately 3 P.M. in the afternoon. It originated in the Turkish area of the city, and it is believed to have started when burning oil spilled from a stove onto a pile of dry straw. Aided by the strong wind and the hot, dry summer weather, the fire quickly spread to the center of the city. It raged for over twenty-four hours and left two-thirds of Salonika in ruins. The fire destroyed over 9,000 buildings – houses, schools, hotels and military offices among them. Over thirty synagogues were destroyed, including the *Italia Yashan* Synagogue. More than 70,000 people were left homeless, among them approximately 50,000 Jews. In the aftermath of the fire, thousands of Saloniki Jews emigrated, moving to Palestine, France and the United States.

There were approximately 55,000 Jews in Salonika at the outbreak of the Second World War. The German army occupied the city on April 8, 1941. Deportations from the city began on March 15, 1943. A total of 54,000 or 97% of the Jews of Salonika perished during the Holocaust.

The city is now called Thessaloniki and is currently home to 1,300 Jews.

# Acknowledgments

I owe a tremendous debt of gratitude to a large number of individuals who gave of their time and expertise at various points during the writing of this book. These people span the globe from London to Salonika and from Toronto to Jerusalem. Their input, advice and guidance were invaluable, and I would like to express my thanks to each of them.

I am deeply indebted to Martin Sugarman, Archivist of the Jewish Museum of the Association of Jewish Ex-Servicemen and Women of the U.K. (AJEX), London, for his unflagging help with Anglo-Jewish military history.

Special thanks go to Jacqueline Gill, London, great-niece of Corporal Israel (Issey) Shibko, a British Jewish soldier who served with the Welsh Regiment and was killed in action in Salonika on September 18, 1918, for supplying me with letters and other documents; Jonathan Grodzinski, Fourth Generation Master Baker, of J. Grodzinski & Daughters, London, for providing me with essential details about the Jewish bakery business at the turn of the twentieth century; and Dolia Asher, nee Perahia, of Jerusalem, for sharing her childhood memories and photographs of Salonika with me.

Erika Perahia Zemour of the Jewish Museum of Thessaloniki, Greece, tirelessly provided me with essential historical and geographical information about Salonika. *"Epharisto para poli."*

My sincere thanks to friends Sara Orenstein and Joy Conway of London, Michal Elran of Rechovot and Yona Goshen Gottstein of Jerusalem, for their help and encouragement during the early stages of this book.

Closer to home, I would like to acknowledge the help of Marcia Haddad Ikonomopoulos, President, The Association of Friends of Greek Jewry, New York. Her assistance and direction were invaluable.

In Toronto, heartfelt thanks go to Lieutenant Colonel Donald G.A. McKenzie, CD, for explaining military structure and procedure; Mrs. Sarita Frasco, for her help with Ladino proverbs and sayings; friend and fellow librarian Lynn Pasternak, for her early reading of the manuscript; and family friend and amateur genealogist Jerrold Landau, for allowing me to "borrow" a branch of his extensive family tree, the Sheinfeld family of Kalarash.

I also wish to thank my editor Roberta Chester for her grace and precision, and Nachum Shapiro, managing editor of Judaica Press, for his professionalism and insight.

My children, Binyamin, Leora, Ari and Tamar, deserve particular mention. They are my first readers and my best listeners, and they are a constant source of inspiration.

*Acharon acharon chaviv.* Thank you, Ira, for teaching me how to use a kaleidoscope.


*Miriam Walfish*
SEPTEMBER 2008